ZEINA
STARBORN
and the EMERALD KING

ALSO BY HANNAH DURKAN

Zeina Starborn and the Sky Whale

ZEINA
STARBORN
and the EMERALD KING

HANNAH DURKAN

Orion
Children's Books

ORION CHILDREN'S BOOKS

First published in Great Britain in 2023 by Hodder & Stoughton

1 3 5 7 9 10 8 6 4 2

Text copyright © Hannah Durkan, 2023
Illustrations copyright © George Ermos, 2023

The moral rights of the author and illustrator have been asserted.

A CIP catalogue record for this book
is available from the British Library.

ISBN 978 1 510 11185 1

Printed and bound in Great Britain by Clays Ltd, Elcograf S.p.A.

The paper and board used in this book are from well-managed
forests and other responsible sources.

Orion Children's Books
An imprint of
Hachette Children's Group
Part of Hodder & Stoughton Limited
Carmelite House
50 Victoria Embankment
London EC4Y 0DZ

An Hachette UK Company
www.hachette.co.uk

www.hachettechildrens.co.uk

For Kieron, Orla and Rowan

THE SMOG SCOOP
Know the truth, trust the revolution

INGENIOUS SMOG RATS EVADE CAPTURE AGAIN!

Last night yet another sky whale was saved by the brave Smog Rats, increasing their total to twenty-five rescued whales in the six months since the legendary liberation of the Willoughby Whale – the world's oldest sky whale hotel. The actions of the ever more desperate lawkeepers are simply no match for the Smog Rats' superior new technology. Guards of the Starlight View Spa Hotel were ambushed by a number of small, lightning-fast and completely silent airships.

'It was amazing!' one steward, who wished to remain anonymous, told our secret reporter. 'One second all was quiet and then suddenly there were Smog Rats everywhere! An alarm sounded telling us to get into the life ships as quickly as possible.

Lawkeepers rushed to help those guarding the STANS room but it was too late – the Smog Rats had already freed the whale from the machine's control.'

Thankfully, there were no fatalities, despite a number of witnesses reporting lawkeepers firing blindly into the evacuating crowds in an attempt to injure Smog Rats. Crucially, the whale also escaped unharmed and is now free and safe. In recent weeks, a number of whale rescue missions have been complicated by the whale's Above 'owners' choosing to attack and injure the creature with harpoons, rather than let it go free.

Belows working in cities across the continent and on airships throughout the Upper Atmosphere are beginning to hope the Smog Rats' success marks a permanent change for good in our society. Recruits to the Smog Rats' noble cause increase every month.

Unfortunately, arrests of Belows by lawkeepers are also on the rise. Driven by fear, and the need for more workers in the mining grounds to replace those liberated by the advancing Kotarth forces in the west, lawkeepers are rounding up Belows in droves, whether or not they are suspected of having Smog Rat links. This publication's message to you is to STAY STRONG. The change is coming. May we all have the courage to do what we know is right.

Pseudonym

CHAPTER 1

A brisk breeze blew a dark tendril of curls across Zeina's face as the *Pine Hawk* ducked beneath the clouds. She tucked it behind her ear, leaning over the airship's railings to examine the landscape below.

In the six months since her and Jackson's adventure with Vivianne Steele, nature had been busy reclaiming the Western Mining Grounds as their own. Vines snaked around the steel struts of abandoned shaft towers, where new shoots, green and bright, broke through blackened-brick chimneys. The long arms of rusted excavators grasped uselessly into the sky and the first nesting birds of the year flew past metal teeth, blissfully unaware that they were making their homes in the jaws of an old ore-crusher.

A few miles back, the *Pine Hawk* had flown high above where the battle still raged between the Kotarth army and lawkeeper forces. Hidden in the smog, Zeina shuddered as the sounds of explosions and pistol fire reached them from the front line below. She was glad that – for now, at least – her dear friend Katu, a Kotarth prince, was too busy working with the Smog Rats to join his brethren. As the Kotarth fought to reclaim their lost lands and the lawkeepers strove to keep control of the ore mines, heavy losses occurred on both sides.

Zeina raised her spyglass, scanning the horizon for any sight of the Smog Rats' airship, the *Nightjar* – her home. At last she spotted it moored atop an abandoned mine, its two magnificent wings raised and folded like a sleeping dragon.

'Ninety degrees towards the starboard bow,' she called to her dad, who was standing at the controls in the cockpit.

'Right you are. Hold on!' he smiled back. Zeina's stomach lurched as the *Pine Hawk* dodged and swerved; despite all his practice, her dad was still a much better innovator than he was a pilot.

The *Pine Hawk* was just one of the four short-range airships they had built from salvaged scrap. Instead of wings, Zeina's dad had designed them to fly using a central rotor. Their three fan-shaped blades sliced through the air, producing only the faintest hum. All the short-range airships – *Pine Hawk, Gold Swift, Oak Hook* and *Owlet* – were lightning-fast and small enough to dock on the deck of the *Nightjar* itself.

Zeina's heart fluttered as they weaved closer. She had been away far too long and missed her crew-mates terribly.

Zeina and her dad had been sent to a secret location to build a sister ship for the *Nightjar*. It had taken them a few weeks, but now the *Osprey* was nearly finished. One more trip back and it would be ready for its maiden voyage to the Southern Continent.

The old Zeina would never, in her wildest dreams, have imagined this life for herself. And yet every time Zeina thought about the *Osprey*, her heart filled with dread. For once it was complete, the crew of the *Nightjar* – her family – would be split in two.

Half would head south on the new airship, hunting down the sky whale hotels that toured during the summer, and the other half would stay behind to continue their work on the western and northern tourist routes. Captain Parr had not yet decided who would go where.

Zeina couldn't bear the thought of spending the long summer months apart from any of her friends. Even now, she fretted every time Shrapnel or Katu went away on a spying mission, and during the short weeks she had spent separated from the crew, terrible imaginings had haunted her.

Had the crew's location been discovered? Had they been caught up in the battle for the mining grounds? Was everyone still alive and safe?

The very real dangers she had faced last year during her adventure with Steele had left a scar on Zeina's soul.

What she worried most about was being separated from Jackson. He had been acting strangely before they left – moody and irritable – the reality of what his Uncle Hamilton had done to them finally dawning on him, Zeina supposed. She and Jackson had been through a lot and, more than anything, they needed each other.

Finally, the deck of the *Nightjar* was directly beneath them. A welcome party craned their heads skywards and waved. Beard grinned at them from the crow's nest, his hand signals guiding them down safely and, although Zeina was pleased to see him, her stomach clenched; Katu would usually be on duty in the crow's nest – he must not be home.

The crew assembled on the deck, standing well back as the *Pine Hawk* swerved and bumped itself into the docking station.

'Your landings are getting much better, Asher!' Captain Parr called up to the cockpit, smiling beneath the brim of her tricorn hat.

'Thank you, Captain,' her dad called back.

It was only once the landing skids had safely made contact with the deck and the rotor blades had stopped completely that Jackson and Sparks raced forward to meet them.

Sparks got to them first, and Zeina spotted that she was

wearing her hair in two braids that she curled into buns, a hairstyle Zeina had shown her how to do before she'd left. Still, little could be done with the halo of shorter white spikes around her forehead that still stood on end, giving her the appearance that she had just been electrocuted. Her large eyes sparkled and she did not need to say a word for Zeina to know exactly what she was saying.

'I've missed you too, Sparks,' Zeina said softly, as the two skinny arms locked themselves around Zeina's middle.

Jackson held back in his usual awkward way, cheeks flushed and a mop of auburn hair covering his eyes. Zeina waved him over and embraced him tightly.

'I suppose I've missed you too, Jackson,' she joked, and when his steel-blue eyes finally met hers, she could tell that the feeling was mutual.

Zeina's dad had descended from the cockpit and was already deep in conversation with Captain Parr. They spoke in low voices, her dad peering darkly over his spectacles. The silver fingers of Parr's mechanical hand stroked her chin thoughtfully and when her one eye, as dark as midnight, caught Zeina watching, she smiled.

'Shrapnel and Katu should be back from their mission tomorrow and then we can celebrate us all being back together with a little party, I think. For now, let's help Asher and Zeina get settled. Sparks, you take these supplies over to

Jamie. Jackson, help Zeina take these boxes down to her workshop, while I catch up with Asher.'

The metallic smell of grease and iron greeted Zeina like a warm hug as she flung open the door to her workshop.

'It's so good to be back,' she said, stroking the rough wood of her workbench and touching each of her tools, as if she were trying to soak everything in.

'Humph.' Jackson heaved the last of the luggage and boxes through the door and collapsed into a chair. 'What's this one?' he asked, regarding a black leather case with some curiosity.

'Oh,' sighed Zeina glumly. 'That's the prototype Dad has asked me to work on while he finishes off the *Osprey*.' She opened the case's small silver clasp, giving Jackson a glimpse of a tangle of wires attached to a bulb and a lens. 'It's solar tech – a way to change energy from the sun into power for our airships.'

'That sounds amazing.' Jackson's eyes lit up with excitement.

'It would be if it worked,' Zeina sulked, snapping the case shut. 'Dad wants it finished before the *Osprey* sets off, but . . . I haven't got very far.'

Zeina found she just couldn't summon the concentration to finish the solar tech. She felt honoured her dad had trusted her with such an important task; however, every time she tried to work on it, her mind was filled with visions of the *Osprey* setting off to the sunny Southern Continent, taking her and her friends far away from each other. The truth was she was dragging her feet, and worse still she had been lying to her dad; he believed that she was on the very brink of success.

'So what's the *Osprey* like?' Jackson asked. 'Is it finished?'

'Nearly . . .' Zeina hesitated. 'It's the same design as the *Nightjar*, just slightly bigger.' She chewed her bottom lip. 'The cabins and the cockpit are finished. We still need to source a little more scrap metal for the wings and Dad is finishing off the short-range airships for the deck. What have I missed here, on the *Nightjar*?'

Jackson rolled his eyes. 'Nothing! Not *one* whale raid since the Starlight View. Just Parr bossing everyone around *as usual*.'

'Jackson!' Zeina laughed. 'She *is* the captain – that's her job!'

Jackson scoffed. Zeina appreciated how frustrated he felt. Since learning about his family's role in the cruel STAN systems that controlled the sky whale hotels, he had been focused entirely on getting rid of every single one. It was what Captain Parr wanted too, but over the last few months they had butted heads often on the speed at which the Smog Rats should be working.

'Parr is your guardian now, Jackson,' Zeina continued gently. 'She only wants the best for you and Sparks. You know that really. It's normal to argue sometimes – just look at me and Dad!'

Jackson's reply was nothing but a grumble.

'Here,' she said brightly. 'I've brought you back a gift from the *Osprey*.'

From a box of tools and scrap metal she fumbled until she reached a stack of neatly folded newspapers tied up with string. 'I've been collecting these for you while I've been away, asking anyone who came to drop off supplies. But if Parr catches you, remember, you *didn't* get them from me.'

She handed him the little pile of newspapers – three copies of *Eastern News Daily*, four copies of the *Ravenport Herald* and no less than five of the new Below newspaper, the *Smog Scoop*, written by the mysterious Pseudonym. Parr disapproved of newspapers. The awful lies printed in the Above papers about the Smog Rats enraged her and yet she found the truths printed in the *Smog Scoop* even more alarming. The captain worried that Pseudonym, whoever they were, gave far too much away. Belows wouldn't be the only ones reading the *Scoop*; lawkeepers would be carefully scouring the text for any clues as to the Smog Rats' whereabouts.

Jackson untied the string, flicking through the papers greedily. 'Aw, thanks, Zeina!'

'Well, I could have brought you back anything from the black market – chocolate, sweets, velocycle parts. But I knew what my good friend Jackson would want most in the world is newspapers!' Her nose wrinkled with amusement. She leaned over his shoulder, reading some of the more ridiculous headlines from the Above newspapers out loud.

INHALING ORE FUMES INCREASES INTELLIGENCE

KOTARTH SOLDIERS EAT PRISONERS

REVEALED: SMOG RATS' PLAN TO STEAL YOUR CHILDREN!

She laughed. 'I'm still not sure why you bother with them. It's all a load of rubbish, except for the *Smog Scoop*, and we don't need to read a paper to find out about the latest whale raids.'

Jackson's eyes scanned the latest issue of the *Smog Scoop*, which outlined the attack on the Starlight View. 'But *we* don't actually get to see any of the action now, do we? Not any more,' he huffed. 'Not since your dad designed those short-range airships.'

Jackson was right. In the months since the triumphant

13

raid of the Willoughby Whale, the invention of the smaller airships had caused a seismic shift in the roles he, Sparks and Zeina played during whale raids. Long gone were the days when the *Nightjar* itself would board the sky whale hotel and everyone would scramble across ladders, overpower lawkeepers, free the whale from its STAN system and then scramble back before the whale bolted.

Now a smaller team of Smog Rats could use these airships to sneak aboard key locations. It was quicker and far less risky; however, someone had to stay behind on the *Nightjar*, hiding in the smog nearby. And, being the youngest members of the crew, it was usually Zeina, Jackson and Sparks left behind. Instead of being part of the action, they made repairs, catalogued supplies, watched the radio and waited.

Zeina hated it, waiting and imagining the dangers their friends could be facing, but she knew in many ways it was worse for Jackson. She, at least, had her inventions to keep her busy. But Jackson sat and seethed. His Uncle Hamilton was still out there aboard a sky whale somewhere – still profiting from his family's cruel technology, still free to enjoy those profits, even after killing Jackson's parents and plotting with Steele to get rid of Jackson.

Something in an issue of the *Ravenport Herald* had caught Jackson's eye. Zeina followed his gaze. Underneath a large article about perfect spring escapes in the Southern Continent was a smaller headline.

HAMILTON WILLOUGHBY WOWS
AT FASHION AWARDS

Next to it was a picture of Hamilton smiling in a particularly ugly hat. Jackson's jaw clenched, his hands shaking as he tore out the article as neatly as he could. Zeina could tell it was taking all his strength not to rip right through his uncle's neck.

'Oh, Jackson. Why torture yourself?' Zeina asked. Perhaps she shouldn't have given him the newspapers after all.

She watched as he retrieved an envelope from the inside pocket of his overalls. He smoothed out the contents, each an article about Hamilton he had collected from stolen newspapers.

WILLOUGHBY FAMILY STRONG IN FACE
OF TRAGEDY

INVESTMENTS IN STANS TECH TRIPLE
DESPITE WHALE ATTACKS

STOCKS RISE THANKS TO HAMILTON
WILLOUGHBY

'I have to know what he's up to, Zeina. Parr promised that we would make him pay, but she hasn't done a thing.' His eyes flickered with rage, making Zeina flinch. 'He's still out there, free, despite everything he did last year. He's still making money off torturing whales, living in luxury!'

'We'll get him, Jackson,' Zeina soothed. 'Parr promised, and we have no reason to doubt her.'

'I should be out there helping,' Jackson breathed. 'Not stuck here reading and cataloguing supplies. I can't stand it, Zeina!'

His face was red and sweating, his chest heaving in short, ragged breaths. This was what Zeina had been worried about. She had been away too long. With no one to open up to, and distract him, Jackson had stewed in his pain. 'It was different when we got to go on the raids – when we were useful to the cause.'

'It might not seem like it, but you *are* helping. What we're doing *is* useful,' Zeina insisted, touching his shoulder gently.

'No, we aren't!' he snapped, startling her into silence. 'Neither of us have done anything to help an actual sky whale in months. All I do is run errands for Parr and you're just an assistant for your dad, like you were back in Ravenport.' His words hit her across the face like an icy slap.

'You should know,' he continued, 'I've asked Parr to join the *Osprey* team. I want to go south – it's our best chance of finding Hamilton. He always goes south for the summer season.'

Zeina felt a twinge in her chest. 'But as your guardian, surely Parr will want to keep you with her?'

She tried not to think about what would happen if she had to stay behind to help her dad. They would be separated for months, if not longer!

Jackson grunted. He wouldn't look her in the eye. She thought about all that time she had spent worrying while she had been apart from him. It hurt that he hadn't even waited to speak to her first before going straight to Parr. 'You don't care about any of us one bit, do you? Finding Hamilton and getting revenge – that's all you care about! Can't you see that it's eating you up?'

She tried to catch his gaze, desperate to help him clamber out of his gloom, but he continued to stubbornly glower down at the newspapers in his hands.

'Well, it's been really lovely catching up with you, Jackson, but this "assistant" had better get back to her pointless work.'

Without another word, he scooped up his newspapers and stormed off, slamming the door behind him.

CHAPTER 2

The new morning brought Jackson little comfort – he and Zeina had stubbornly avoided each other since their fight. Finding a patch of sunlight, Jackson furtively looked around, but the deck of the *Nightjar* was quite abandoned. Everyone was busy. He exhaled, taking out an issue of the *Smog Scoop* and flicking through the pages. It felt good to be going against Parr's orders. A tiny rebellion.

Pseudonym was a bit of a hero to Jackson. It was the fact that they told the world the truth about Hamilton and the STAN system, the fact that they wrote about the Smog Rats' victories even though Captain Parr forbade it. Jackson wished he was doing half as much.

The feeling that he was being watched crept up on Jackson, making the back of his neck tingle. He whirled around, tucking the newspaper behind his back in a sharp, noisy rustle.

'Oh, Sparks!' he breathed. 'I thought you were Parr.'

She smiled, shaking her head as she stepped out from behind a barrel of fish guts. Her large eyes took in the crumple of newsprint.

'It's the new issue,' he replied, beckoning her over to read next to him.

Their eyes scanned the page in unison. Sparks reached inside her overalls, retrieving the little pad of paper and pencil she had become accustomed to always carrying with her. She still had not said one word about what had happened to her before Parr and Jamie had found her terrified and alone, locked inside the STANS room of a whale hotel. Although she seemed to grow a little in confidence every day, it was only Jamie or Shrapnel that she would talk to directly, whispering what she wanted to say close to their ears. She wrote carefully in clear, neat capitals, holding the paper up for Jackson to read when she had finished.

PARR ISN'T GOING TO LIKE THIS.

'No,' agreed Jackson. 'Parr isn't going to like this at all.'

'What exactly am I not going to like?' The voice of Captain Parr rang out, making them both turn quickly. She would often appear like this, as if from nowhere – a consequence of being an outlaw for so long, Jackson supposed. He shoved the paper behind his back once again, but much too late for Parr to miss. Despite having only one eye, she did not miss anything.

'Come on, hand it over. You know full well that I don't allow *that* garbage on *my* ship.'

Jackson sulked, placing it in the metallic outstretched palm of her mechanical hand. She frowned, her cheeks flushing as she crumpled the paper up and shoved it into the pocket of her brocade jacket, much to Jackson's annoyance.

'I hadn't finished that,' he growled. A flame of anger, always so close to the surface it seemed these days, flushed his cheeks. 'At least Pseudonym is writing the *truth*. Unlike the *Herald*, which prints all those awful lies about us. Why shouldn't everyone know about the good the Smog Rats are doing? Imagine that paper falling through the smog to the Belows trapped in cities like Ravenport.'

'I have explained the dangers *many times*, Jackson. Pseudonym gives far too much away – they place Smog Rats in real danger. I expect my orders to be followed. By *everyone*,' Parr said pointedly. 'I am your captain first, and your guardian second.'

Sparks hung her head, her fingers twisting nervously around her notepad and pencil. In many ways, Jackson loved the fact that Captain Parr had wanted to take on guardianship of him and Sparks until they came of age; he trusted her more than any adult he had ever known. Yet having a fearsome sky pirate captain be responsible for you certainly had its downsides. She expected obedience and was used to getting her own way.

'Now, I thought you'd be spending time with Zeina?' Her eye narrowed on him sharply.

'We aren't talking,' Jackson admitted.

Sparks frowned and began to scribble.

BUT YOU MISSED HER SO MUCH WHEN SHE WAS AWAY.

'I agree, Sparks,' Captain Parr sighed. 'I just don't understand. You spent weeks moping about, waiting for her to come back and then within moments you're not even on speaking terms! What caused the falling-out?'

'It was about the *Osprey*,' he grumbled. 'About who would go south.'

'Well, what a ridiculous thing to argue about,' Parr replied. 'Especially seeing as neither of you have any say at all in where I send my crew. Now, go and make up with her.'

'But—'

'That's an order from your captain, lad. I can't stand all this sulking about. Besides, Asher needs Zeina to concentrate on finishing the solar tech, not mourning over a silly fight with you. Go on – off with you.'

As he approached Zeina's workshop, any nerves Jackson felt were rapidly replaced by panic as a large explosion inside billowed thick black smoke from around the doorway. He heard Zeina shriek and then the door swung open violently.

'SAND!' she yelled, her face covered in black smudges. Behind her, Jackson could see a small fire burning a hole into her workbench.

He reached for the emergency bucket she kept in the corridor and passed it to her.

She flung it over the experiment, the sand extinguishing the flames just in time to stop them from licking up the curtains.

'What was that?' he asked, as she opened her porthole window to waft out the gathering smoke.

'Oh, well, I *could* tell you, but since I'm *nothing but an assistant*, I'm not sure it's my place,' she griped.

'Yeah, about that.' Jackson looked down at his hands, twisting them nervously. 'I'm really sorry, Zeina. I don't know what got into me yesterday. The truth is, it's been awful, you not being here these last few weeks—'

She swallowed him up in her arms before he could even finish, and he breathed in the scent of smoke and grease from her overalls, feeling instantly better.

'It's OK, I missed you too.' She smiled. 'Come on, I've been desperate to show you this. Might not look like much at the moment, but this is going to change the world!'

She gestured to the smouldering bench where a twist of burnt wires smoked around a broken lightbulb. Jackson's eyebrows raised and he nodded kindly, doing his best to seem impressed. Zeina laughed.

'This lens here captures energy from the sun and turns it into power for the lightbulb. It's a prototype for solar technology that we could use to power the airships in low-smog zones. It would give Beard and the others a break from cycling. Very useful on the sunny Southern Continent.'

'Great! When will it be finished?'

'If my dad asks? Any day now,' Zeina said. 'At the moment it's still a little bit . . . temperamental. But now we're all back together, I'm sure I'll be able to concentrate on getting it finished.'

The sharp blast of a whistle above signalled that an airship was incoming.

'That'll be Katu and Shrapnel!' Zeina grinned. 'Come on!'

They ran up the stairs to the deck and were met with a crowd of Smog Rats, necks craned towards the cloudless sky. Zeina muscled their way through until Jackson could see the black speck of an airship against the blue.

'Starboard, Captain. It looks like the *Gold Swift*,' called down Beard from the crow's nest.

'Thanks, Beard.' Captain Parr raised her own spyglass. 'Asher, direct them into the docking station once they get a little closer.'

It still felt a little strange for Jackson to hear Zeina's dad being called by his first name. In the last six months Jackson had had to train himself out of calling him Mr Starborn – something he still did on occasions, much to Zeina's amusement.

'I can't wait,' Zeina said. 'I've been so worried about them. Shrapnel is sure to be full of gossip too.'

Something occurred to Jackson.

'You don't think *he* could be Pseudonym, do you?' Jackson whispered.

'Huh?'

'Shrapnel? Could he be Pseudonym?'

Zeina scoffed. 'Shrapnel's no writer! And anyway, there's no way he would keep that from Parr. He's too scared of her.'

Jackson's thoughts were broken by another yell from Beard. 'Looks like they might be in trouble, Captain! I can see smoke.'

Indeed, as Jackson squinted up into the sky he could now see the tiny ship was zigzagging wildly across the clouds. Smoke billowed from an enormous hole in the *Gold Swift*'s smog chamber and both of its cycles were being pedalled frantically to keep it up in the air.

The *Gold Swift* swerved closer and closer, Jackson's heartbeat quickening with every lurch. Zeina grabbed Jackson's hand, her fingers trembling, and it was only once her dad had safely guided the ship down on to the deck that she relaxed. Jackson watched as Zeina ran forward into the smoke even before the rotor blades had stopped completely. She started to climb up into the cockpit, when a large leather travelling bag was shoved out of the cockpit door, landing in Zeina's outstretched arms with a thud that sent her to the floor.

'Ow!'

Jackson rushed forward to help.

A voice that was most definitely *not* Shrapnel's or Katu's called down from the cockpit. 'Oh, sorry!'

A pair of elegant patent-leather ankle boots emerged, followed by a cloud of lace skirts and the bodice and shoulders of a woman – an Above woman, no less.

CHAPTER 3

Zeina reeled. Who was this Above? And more importantly *where* were Shrapnel and Katu? The woman landed on the deck, retrieving her bag from Zeina, who stared up at her in furious confusion.

'Thank you so much for catching my bag!' The lady smiled handsomely. 'I've wanted to see the *Nightjar* for ages!' she exclaimed, looking around at the crew, who were all staring at her. Zeina felt the strong arms of her dad lift her from the floor and set her on her feet.

Zeina could now appreciate how young the woman was – maybe only a year or two older than Shrapnel. Zeina also realised she wasn't as put together as she had first seemed. Her bouffant blonde hair escaped from underneath an askew feathered bonnet and her powdered face was smudged in places.

'Stand down, everyone,' Shrapnel called down. 'This is Ned!'

'It's Nedra, actually.' The girl smiled, offering her hand to Zeina, who ignored it, rubbing her arm where it had hit the floor. Captain Parr lowered the pistol she had raised.

'You could have come out first, Shrapnel,' she grumbled. 'Nedra's outfit gave us quite a scare!'

'Sorry, Parr,' Shrapnel replied, as he limped a little down the steps. His injury had healed considerably well but was still giving him trouble. 'I didn't think.'

'I must apologise, Nedra,' the captain said, striding forward to take her hand. 'I've heard so much about you and it's good to finally meet you in person.'

Zeina was gripped by a sudden nausea – the cockpit was now empty.

'Where's Katu?' she growled, squaring up to Shrapnel. 'You *promised* you'd stay together.'

'All right, Zee,' Shrapnel grinned. 'Nice to see you too! Don't worry, Katu's fine!'

'It was my fault, I'm afraid,' Nedra piped up from behind him, as Zeina shot her a scowl.

Shrapnel continued. 'We got a distress call from Ned. She'd got into trouble on her spying mission, so I offered to go and pick her up. Katu was right behind us in the *Owlet* when we were spotted by a lawkeeper's ship. The *Owlet* had time to hide in the smog but our smog chamber was hit so Ned and I had to resort to cycle power to escape.' Before anyone could ask, he added, 'It's all right – we managed to shake them off more than ten miles back.'

'It's for situations just like this one that the solar tech will be *invaluable*,' Zeina's dad said. The reminder made her chest feel heavy.

Beard was waving in the second airship now. The *Owlet* landed much more delicately than the *Gold Swift*, and when the door opened Zeina was relieved to see Katu descend the ladder in one fluid cat-like movement.

'OOUFF!' All Katu's fur stood up on end as she embraced him tightly. Zeina let go, remembering Katu didn't like being hugged, and he held out his paw to be stroked instead.

'Hello, Zeina,' he said, pink tongue curling round his sharp teeth. 'It's good to see you too!' He looked around with a small smile. 'It's so lovely for us all to be back together again. But, Parr, I must steal you away for a moment. There is a matter we need to discuss.'

A glimmer of light from above transformed into a beautiful white bird, as Albi – an ice raven – landed gracefully on Katu's shoulder. Ruffling his wings and flexing his claws, Albi let out an ugly croak that made Katu's pointed ears flick.

'Yes, yes, I know,' he said, giving Albi a biscuit, which sent crumbs cascading down the shoulder of his black travelling cloak. Katu growled softly in annoyance, brushing them away, before carefully removing a small scroll from his top

28

pocket. It was the same size as the ones he attached to Albi's leg when he wanted to send a message, but this one was made of a green iridescent paper and tied with tiny loop of golden thread. Katu passed the scroll to Parr as they strode away towards her cabin, another biscuit for a cawing Albi in his other paw.

'What's that about?' Zeina asked her dad in a whisper.

'Never you mind,' he replied, ruffling the top of her head. 'It's time for you to get back to that prototype! I'll make a start on repairing the *Gold Swift*'s smog chamber and then I'll be along to your workshop so you can show me the progress you've made.'

Zeina hoped he didn't notice her gulp as he kissed the top of her head and said goodbye.

Shrapnel, Sparks and Jackson were all crowded around Nedra, laughing and applauding. Zeina saw that the leather travelling bag, which had been so rudely dropped on her, was now open and had expanded to at least four times the size. Unfolded from the centre was a full-length wardrobe with an array of strange outfits – Above suits and lace dresses, smudged overalls, steward uniforms, aviator jackets, even a dark-green lawkeeper's outfit. From little golden hooks hung a wall of wigs in any colour you could imagine. Long ones, short ones, braids and ornately styled up-dos. From the bottom of the bag, two drawers had popped forward, one

29

filled with hats and the other with props – glasses, moustaches, scarves and jewellery.

Nedra was turning away from the group, pulling various items out of the bag, throwing them on and then turning back to face them in character. Zeina watched as she disappeared behind a row of wigs and was replaced by an image of the perfect Above gentleman – coiffed hair, top hat and monocle.

'Good evening, my dears,' she said in a voice that sounded frighteningly like Hamilton Willoughby. 'And isn't it a fine evening! Won't you all join me for dinner in my penthouse?'

Jackson looked rather disturbed, but Shrapnel guffawed. 'Didn't I tell you? She's a master of disguise!'

She disappeared again and this time when she turned back she was wearing a short black wig and lawkeeper's hat, face distorted into an evil grimace. 'To the mining grounds for all of you!' she spat in a voice quite unlike her own. She held a truncheon up to Sparks, who hid behind Shrapnel until Nedra started pulling silly faces to make her laugh.

Finally she took off her disguise to reveal hair shorter than either Shrapnel's or Jackson's.

'Easier for the wigs,' she explained when she spotted Zeina staring. Zeina was amazed. When her face became her own,

30

Nedra looked friendly enough, but it was disconcerting how quickly she could change her expression and become someone else entirely.

'Ned, you can meet Zee properly now she's not too busy trying to kill me.' Shrapnel glared at Zeina. 'Zee, this is Ned, one of our newest recruits, liberated from the Western Mining Grounds and, as you can see, a very talented con-artist!'

'Hello,' Nedra smiled. 'I'm so sorry my bag landed on you! I've been undercover as Lady Bellingham the Fifth for a fortnight and it seems to have rather rubbed off on me.'

'Someone started asking questions,' Shrapnel explained, 'and she had to make a quick exit.'

'Who would have thought there was an actual Lady Bellingham and that she had a cousin aboard?' Nedra shook her head. 'Good job you guys were nearby!'

Captain Parr marched from the cockpit, the green scroll clasped in her hand and Katu trailing close behind.

'We're setting off north *immediately*,' she announced to the crew on the deck. 'Katu has had a message from Palik – the new king has invited a group of us to attend their spring Equinox celebrations.'

'What in the world is an Equinox?' asked Shrapnel.

'The spring Equinox is a celebration the Feln hold each year to mark the return of the sun after their long, dark winter,' Katu explained. 'The King of Palik holds a grand party in the Glacial Palace every year in its honour.'

'Never heard of it,' Shrapnel said. 'Wasn't covered in our school, was it, Zee?'

Zeina shook her head. Her months with the Smog Rats had filled in some of the gaps left by her Below education, which had focused more on learning to follow instructions and less about understanding their world.

She now knew that the Feln were a relation of the Kotarth, that they lived on the Northern Continent, and that they found the term 'Ice Bears' incredibly offensive – a name invented by Vivianne Steele when she 'discovered' them.

There were also the sandy-haired, fox-like creatures called the Zugmi on the Southern Continent, or at least there had been until humans had polluted it so badly that it became a barren desert.

'We are to travel first to Palik and then await further instructions,' continued Parr. 'The exact location of the Glacial Palace changes every winter and is a closely guarded secret. It is completely rebuilt each year, out of giant blocks of ice from their frozen lakes.'

Zeina's fingertips tingled. Ever since she had read about Vivianne Steele's expedition north, she had been desperate to see Palik. It would be risky crossing the northern tourist route at this time of year, but at least they would all be together.

'What about rescuing sky whales?' Jackson brooded, his face like a storm. 'What does the king even want with us?'

'Hopefully to join forces, Jackson,' Parr replied. 'We won't know for certain until we get there, but it is *vital* that we go.'

'We have our . . . differences,' Katu growled. 'But you can be sure that the Feln find the treatment of sky whales by Aboves every bit as disgusting as we do. The last king supported us – from a distance – but now a new king has the throne, we need to make sure he is on our side. Hopefully he will agree to form an alliance with us.'

'And we'll *all* get to go to the palace?' Zeina asked. She was already worrying about what would happen once the *Nightjar* reached Palik. She knew they could not leave the airship completely abandoned and she didn't like the thought of being separated from her friends so soon after they had been reunited.

'Once there, I will decide who will make the journey to the palace. But you can be sure it won't be anyone *standing about idly* while there's work to be done!' Parr glared pointedly at the children crowded around Nedra and her bag. 'Everyone to their posts. The Equinox is only a week away and we'll have to make good time if we hope to make it to Palik on schedule.'

As Parr marched towards the cockpit, the crew leapt into action. Shrapnel grabbed Jackson to help him unload supplies, Sparks scampered off to her radio room and Zeina was trying to think of an excuse to avoid the mess in her cabin.

'Shrapnel's told me you're a bit of a hero, you know,' said Nedra, startling Zeina out of her thoughts.

'*Shrapnel* said that?' Zeina watched her wipe the powder from her face and unclip a long string of pearls from her neck.

'Well, not exactly! But I can tell that's what he thinks. You really are amazing – beating Vivianne Steele, freeing that baby whale, inventing the aerocycle.'

Zeina blushed.

'You know, I would still be in the mining grounds if Steele wasn't dead.' Nedra's grey eyes grew dark for a moment, haunted by memories that lingered like smoke. She shook her head and smiled. 'It's thanks to you that I'm free.'

Zeina shrugged, shuffling uncomfortably where she stood. She wasn't sure why this stranger was heaping all this praise on to her – what exactly had Shrapnel told her? 'Well, it wasn't quite—'

'And Shrap says that you're inventing *more* new technology with your dad?' Nedra interrupted, focusing again on her own image in the mirror as she wiped the smudged make-up from around her eyes.

There was a sinking feeling in Zeina's stomach. 'Well, that's nowhere near finished yet,' she admitted quietly.

'Oh, I'm sure if the amazing Zeina Starborn can't get it finished then no one can! You'll find it easier now you're back home on the *Nightjar*, I would think?'

'Maybe.' Zeina looked down miserably. She thought about her dad's words. He said he'd come to her workshop later to examine her 'progress'. He would be so disappointed. 'I just can't seem to concentrate,' she admitted. 'I've been worrying a lot. Especially when we aren't all together.' The words spilled out of her mouth before she could stop herself. 'I just wish we could all . . . stay together,' Zeina stuttered, and to her horror she felt the telltale pricking of tears. Nedra stopped taking off her make-up for a second and looked very hard at Zeina's reflection in the mirror.

'It must be horrible when the people you love are away from you and you're never sure if they are in danger. I don't know what that's like, really – not any more, anyway.'

'Have you been on your own for long?' Zeina asked, looking away and sniffing, as she wiped at her eyes.

'It feels like it,' Nedra replied, sitting back against the railings with a half-powdered face. 'I never knew my father, and then my mother, she—'

Her voice cracked and Zeina's heart ached; she too knew what it was like to lose a mother. Nedra stopped, unable to finish her sentence. Zeina came to sit beside her, fumbling for words.

Nedra turned to her and smiled. 'It sounds like what you need is a break. Somewhere you can relax, knowing everyone is safe for a while. The Equinox celebrations at the Glacial Palace would be perfect! That's if you can manage to persuade Parr to take you all?'

'Won't it be dangerous?' Zeina asked.

'No! Once you're there, it'll probably be one of the safest places in the four continents. The location of the palace is top secret and you'd be the only humans around for a hundred miles. Airships aren't allowed north of Palik, so there'd be no chance of bumping into lawkeepers, that's for sure.'

'Dad will never agree,' Zeina sulked. 'He'll want me to stay on the *Nightjar* and finish my prototype. In fact, when he sees how far I've got, I doubt he'll even let me out of my workshop.'

Nedra frowned. 'Could you take everything you need with you?'

Zeina nodded. 'I could, I suppose. The prototype is designed to be portable.'

'Couldn't you just . . . *not* show him?' A cheeky grin lit up Nedra's face and Zeina could see why she and Shrapnel got on so well. 'If you tell him it's nearly done but you want to finish it by yourself as a *surprise*? You could tell him you'll unveil it at the Equinox celebrations. That would buy you at least a week to finish it.'

Zeina nodded slowly. A break *was* just what she needed – what they all needed. She was sure she'd be able to finish the solar tech once they were all there, together and safe.

'Thanks, Nedra,' Zeina smiled, feeling a lightness in her chest that had been missing for weeks.

'You're welcome!' Nedra grinned, folding her clothes and wigs back into her bag before she began rubbing once again at the powdered half of her face. 'Hey, if you manage it, try and get me an invite too, OK? I've always wanted to see the famous frozen palace of the Feln.'

CHAPTER 4

The moonlight illuminated a giant, tail-shaped shadow sailing above them, somewhere beyond the smog. It had taken the *Nightjar* two days and two nights to reach the Northern Continent and this was their *second* close call. Reports of a sky whale hotel near the Western Border had sent them into hiding in the mountains yesterday, much to Jackson's disgust, and now this.

'We should be going after it,' Jackson grumbled through his respirator, 'not hiding down here in the smog.'

Kind-hearted Jamie placed a giant hand on Jackson's shoulder and gave it a squeeze. 'I know it's tough, Jackson. I don't like seeing them any more than you do. Parr will have us back to freeing them as soon as possible.'

Jackson grunted.

'Parr feels our meeting with the king takes precedence for now,' Katu whispered calmly. 'And it is not for *any* of us,' his golden crescent eyes narrowed on Jackson, 'to agree or disagree with our captain. If we can form an alliance with the Feln, it will be a great victory for our cause.'

Jackson frowned in frustration as the shadow faded, followed by the whirr of accompanying airships – its guard of lawkeepers. The thought of the poor whale being held captive by his family's STAN system repulsed Jackson. He would not rest until every single one was destroyed. He had even asked Jamie if he would train him up so that one day he might dismantle them on real whale raids.

Although the Willoughby Whale was now free, his uncle still owned the rights to the STANS technology and was profiting off every sky whale hotel still in operation. Jackson knew that at this time of year, Hamilton and Herbert, Jackson's spoilt cousin, would be sunning themselves on a sky whale hotel somewhere on the Southern Continent. He dreamed of finding them – and making them pay. And yet he was sure Captain Parr had already decided he would have to stay behind with her on the *Nightjar*, rather than join the *Osprey* team.

The *Nightjar* fell completely silent – as if the whole crew were holding their breath – until the echoes of the lawkeepers' airships passed. After a signal from Parr, the crew returned to their posts and the *Nightjar* continued its long journey north.

By the time they reached the Palik region, the sun had risen in the east, large and low, and was already beginning to dip behind the mountains to the west. Its glow painted the sky gold. Jackson released himself from his respirator and goggles, his face cooled by the crisp, fresh air.

There were pictures of this part of the Northern Continent in Jackson's textbooks back in Ravenport, but nothing could have prepared him for its breathtaking beauty in real life. A silvery carpet of snow glittered below them in the golden light. Lengthening shadows of evergreens, their branches laden with ice, stippled the mountainsides. The mountaintops were covered in a delicate dusting that reminded Jackson of cakes covered in icing sugar. They flew over a frozen lake, as dark as ink, crystal cracks forming a pattern across its surface that was eerily beautiful.

'Why is the sun so low in the sky?' Zeina squinted. 'It's far too early for sunset, isn't it?' She tapped the glass of a small pocket watch she had attached to a leather strap around her wrist to stop her from losing it.

'Not this far north,' Jackson explained. 'The sun doesn't rise at all for months during winter. That's right, isn't it, Katu?'

'Correct, Jackson. Before this month began, the sun hadn't risen here for *five* whole months. The Feln call this month Valco Sol, which roughly translates as "Welcome, Sun". It is the month in which the Feln welcome back the sun after five whole months of night.'

'The sun doesn't rise for *five* months?' exclaimed Zeina.

'That's right. It rises for just a matter of minutes on the first day of Valco Sol, but the days get progressively longer throughout the month. In the middle of the month is the spring Equinox, when there are exactly twelve hours of sunlight. After the Equinox the days continue to get longer until the last day of Valco Sol, when the sun doesn't set. That marks the beginning of the Feln summer, when the sun stays above the horizon for five whole months,' explained Katu.

'Five months of daytime?' Zeina asked, her head shaking in disbelief.

'You could put it that way, I suppose,' continued Katu. 'There's the month of Valco Nox, or "Welcome, Night", in the autumn, where the opposite happens. The Feln have lots of celebrations throughout the months of Valco Sol and Valco Nox, but the biggest by far is the spring Equinox – we are very lucky to be here for this special time in their calendar.'

'When is the Equinox exactly?' asked Jackson.

'It's just a few days away now,' Katu replied. 'When the sun rises on the Equinox, the main celebrations will begin at the Glacial Palace. Every Feln in the region goes to the palace to eat and drink and celebrate the sun.'

'You don't sound too excited, Katu,' Zeina joked.

'The Kotarth do not enjoy the excesses of parties; it's one of the ways in which we differ from our Feln cousins.' His ears flicked and nostrils flared. 'However, this trip is in the interests of *diplomacy* rather than enjoyment. Whoever is chosen to accompany Parr should feel honoured – it is exceptionally rare for outsiders to be invited to see the Glacial Palace, let alone during the Equinox celebrations. The palace will melt by the end of Valco Sol and won't be rebuilt again until after the month of Valco Nox.'

There was a crackle from the short-range radio Katu carried inside his cloak.

'Katu . . . I saw Albi through my porthole . . . out to starboard . . .'

It was still a little strange hearing Sparks's voice, but recently she had begun to use it more and more. As well as whispering to Jamie and to Shrapnel – who she found particularly amusing – she would also speak through her radio to most members of the crew, as long as she was alone and unobserved in her workshop.

'Thank you, Sparks,' Katu said back into the receiver. 'That'll be our message back from the king, hopefully,' he added, before hurrying away.

Jackson looked at Zeina, who was frowning, her freckled nose scrunched up the way it always was when she was really thinking hard about something. 'You could always ask Sparks for help with your solar tech?' Jackson suggested cautiously. 'She's a real whizz with anything that has wires.'

'I don't *need* help, thank you, Jackson!' Zeina blushed. 'I just need a few more days, that's all. By the time we're celebrating the Equinox, I'll have cracked it.'

'That's if we all go . . .' Jackson trailed off. Surely some of them would have to start preparations for the *Osprey*'s journey south? Part of Jackson hoped the distraction provided by this trip might give him a break from Parr's attention. Maybe she would change her mind about letting him go south.

Captain Parr emerged from the cockpit with Katu and Albi. She demanded their attention, a small green scroll in her hand.

'Good news! The king has sent us his instructions. As airships are forbidden north of Palik City, we are to meet our guide there and they will show us the way to the Glacial Palace by land.'

She looked around, her eye resting on Jackson a little longer than the others. 'After some consideration, the party will include myself, Katu, Zeina, Jackson, Shrapnel, Sparks and Asher.' The children celebrated and Zeina's dad nodded. 'Jamie, Beard and the rest of the crew will stay in Palik to keep a lookout and ensure the *Nightjar* remains hidden. There shouldn't be any lawkeepers this far north, but we can never be too careful.'

'Another week without any whale raids then?' Jackson asked, and he could not help the sharp edge in his tone when

43

he spoke. 'Shouldn't Jamie be busy training one of us to dismantle a STAN system for the *Osprey* mission, rather than hiding in the *Nightjar*?'

Jamie flushed, shaking his head ever so slightly at Jackson.

Parr frowned. 'The *Osprey*'s journey south is on hold for now.'

'WHAT?' Jackson gasped, a hush echoing around the assembled crew.

'Jackson,' Parr spoke firmly. 'If we are going to beat the Above families once and for all, we need an alliance with the Feln. We must meet this new king, impress him and get him on our side.'

A muscle flicked in Jackson's jaw but he said nothing. It would do no good to fight with Parr in front of everybody.

'Katu will represent the Kotarth in the negotiations,' Parr explained, turning back to the rest of the team. 'Asher and Zeina can show off their innovations – the aerocycles and our new solar tech. Your dad tells me you're confident it'll be finished by the end of the week, Zeina?'

Zeina nodded vigorously, but Jackson spotted the telltale flush of her cheeks.

'Good,' Parr said, before turning back to Jackson. 'You and Sparks will come along too. Perhaps you might even *enjoy* yourself, lad? Exploring a top-secret ice palace, seeing the famous Equinox celebrations?' Her eyebrow raised hopefully. 'Shrapnel will come to keep an eye on you all when Asher, Katu and I are busy.'

The crisp air did nothing to cool the fury coursing through Jackson's veins. Shrapnel was only fourteen, yet he was treated like a full adult member of the Smog Rats, and now apparently was also his *babysitter*!

'Don't take it personally, kids,' Shrapnel said, throwing one arm around Zeina's shoulders and the other around Jackson's. 'I'd been looking after myself long before either of you had ever even seen the Upper Atmosphere.'

He laughed as Zeina shoved him off.

'Can Nedra come too?' she asked hopefully.

Parr considered Nedra, who gave her most helpful-looking smile in return.

'I don't see why not.'

Zeina, Shrapnel and Sparks celebrated with Nedra but Jackson frowned at Parr. How could she put everything on hold while Hamilton was still free and whales were still suffering? The captain returned his gaze, coming over and crouching down so that her eye was level with his.

'It's a *week*, lad, that's all. Then we get straight back to doing what we do best, I promise.'

The smile she gave him was so full of hope that he wished he could return it, but his disappointment wouldn't let him. Parr sighed, then raised her voice so the whole crew could hear.

'Palik is on the horizon now, so everyone back to work. And you lot,' she turned to quiet Zeina and the others, who were gabbling with excitement, 'get on your thickest coats and gather your things together – quickly, before I change my mind.'

The *Nightjar* landed in a valley, surrounded on all sides by black jagged mountains and warmed by the rainbow hues of the setting sun. Ice nipped their faces as they climbed down the gangway, wrapped in thick woollen coats. Zeina struggled, hampered by her bulging backpack, tool belt and the leather case that contained her prototype. She refused help from both Jackson and Shrapnel until Parr insisted.

'Palik is at least a mile from here, Zeina, and you'll never make it carrying all that by yourself in all this snow. Nothing wrong with asking for help when it's needed, you know.'

'Come on, Zeina, give me your aerocycle at least,' Jackson said, taking the large golden tube of the folded contraption and putting it beside his, inside his backpack.

'Why are you bringing those?' Shrapnel scoffed. 'Will their smog chambers even work up here?'

Shrapnel had a point; there was far too little smog in the atmosphere this far north. However, Jackson, like Zeina, carried his aerocycle everywhere with him – it made him feel safe.

'I bet Zeina is going to invent a solar-powered one. Aren't you, Zee?' Nedra winked, making Zeina flush beetroot.

From the frozen valley, they waved off the *Nightjar*. Jamie waved back from the cockpit, Beard and the others frantically cycling underneath to make the airship ascend. It disappeared into the sea of clouds that swirled about the mountain peaks and Jackson hoped they would stay safe and hidden.

They started a steady trek up a winding, narrow mountain pass, Albi hovering overhead. Jackson was expecting Palik to be a simple collection of cave dwellings, as this is what all his textbooks back in Ravenport had suggested. He was taken aback when they eventually rounded a corner and were presented with magnificent views of an imposing castle city carved into the black rock of the mountainside. Ornate stone arches bridged the gaps between one mountain cliff and the next and led to a gatehouse, guarded by two enormous statues of Feln warriors. With icicles hanging from their noses, paws and spears, and a layer of white covering their ears and helmets, they looked like giants frozen in time. Beyond them, the cliff face was a maze of windows, doorways, terraces and pillars, all decorated with intricate patterns carved into the stone.

Jackson must have let his surprise show, as Katu looked down at him, speaking with a purr of amusement. 'Not what you imagined, Jackson? Or you, Zeina?' he added, and indeed Zeina's eyes were also wide with wonder.

'But—The newspaper had pictures of Steele discovering Palik, and in those it was just some caves.'

'Well, that will be because that's what Steele chose to show you.' Katu's whiskers bristled. 'It is easier to "discover" places and take home their treasures when you think the beings that live there are somehow *less* than you. If the newspapers had shown you what Palik and the Feln were really like, some people might have started to consider it stealing.'

Jackson gulped, distinctly remembering a large ruby from Palik that was displayed on a table in the entranceway to his old home back in Willoughby Towers – his father had bought it from Steele. He could remember his father bragging about having a piece of the 'Ice Bears' treasure.

'Some of the fortifications are new,' Katu continued, 'but most of this architecture has been here for thousands of years and there were Feln living within the cave system inside that mountain long before humans had learned to walk on two legs.'

He pointed up towards the heads of the magnificent statues. 'You see there are gaps everywhere in the carvings. At one time every one of those spaces was filled with a stone – rubies, sapphires, diamonds and, most importantly, *emeralds*: the sacred stone of the Feln. This valley once glittered with jewels, before Steele plundered it for profit.'

A frosty silence descended on the group as they entered the gatehouse. At first it appeared to be completely deserted. The ebony walls stretched up into a domed ceiling, decorated with carvings of Feln warriors prowling around large circular skylights.

A sudden darkness fell and the room echoed with snarls. Six Feln jumped through the skylights, landing on four paws with gentle thuds. One more blocked the entranceway and another the exit to the city. They were completely surrounded. Each warrior stood taller even than Katu and was easily twice as broad. Heavily armoured and holding golden spears, they advanced on the group, pushing them into the very centre of the circular hall.

'And *who* might you be?' the largest roared into Parr's face, sniffing at her in disgust. 'Humans? HUMANS daring to come back to our city?' He shoved her roughly, his eyes piercingly black against his white fur. His helmet was larger than the others, decorated with carvings and stones to signify his superior rank.

'We have been invited,' Parr replied, her eye fixed determinedly up into his. She handed him the green scroll Albi had delivered to Katu, but the warrior did not take it.

Jackson held his breath, sure that they were about to be attacked. He knew that Parr had told everyone to leave their pistols on the ship but hoped she had at least kept the dagger she hid inside the workings of her mechanical arm. He felt Zeina's quick breath warm against his cold cheek and was sure he could hear her heart hammering in time with his own.

The Feln reached out and grabbed Parr by the shoulder with one enormous clawed paw. He seemed almost double her size and it scared Jackson to see her looking so unusually vulnerable. He bowed over her, lips bared to show dagger teeth.

CHAPTER 5

And just when Zeina was sure that the fearsome warrior was about to attack, swallowing Captain Parr up in one enormous bite – he began to laugh. A coarse, roaring bellow that echoed around the gatehouse chamber. He winked at Parr, grabbing her hand to shake it heartily while all around them growls and snarls changed into great thundering laughter.

'You looked worried for a second there, Captain Parr,' the Feln warrior growled. 'We Feln don't get many visitors – particularly *human* ones. We must be afforded our fun, don't you agree?'

'Of course,' Captain Parr replied. 'But you must excuse me, for though you know my name, I am still unaware of yours.' And although she smiled, each of her words felt carefully measured.

'I am Commander Hugrak, head of the king's guard.' His eyes glinted with mistrust. 'Greetings to you all, humans.

And to you, cousin Katu!' He slapped Katu on the back with just a little too much force, sending Albi squawking and cawing from his shoulder.

'Yes, I do apologise, Captain Parr,' Katu growled. 'I had forgotten how much the Feln pride themselves on their sense of humour.'

'Come, come.' Commander Hugrak wrapped one giant furry arm around Parr and the other around a rather terrified-looking Jackson. 'Give my guards your luggage and we shall escort you to the city. There's not enough sunlight left to make the journey to the palace today, but as soon as the sun rises tomorrow we will set off. Better to rest tonight anyway; the palace is the furthest north it has ever been, so you will need your strength!'

Despite the freezing temperatures, Zeina felt Palik was one of the warmest places she had ever visited. The narrow walkways jostled with busy Feln of all ages. Golden decorations in the shape of the sun and the moon hung from every terrace and doorway. Green and gold flags waved from windows and rooftops – each decorated with the emblem of the Equinox: the outline of a palace, split in two by a moon and a sun. Although there were undoubtedly looks of suspicion by some, many of the residents seemed simply curious, and excited by their strange guests. Shopkeepers waved at them from their kiosks, laden with all manner of strange-looking foods, and younger Feln peeped from doorways, whispering to each other before any one was brave enough to wave at the visitors. Zeina even spotted copies of the *Smog Scoop* on sale – a sure-fire sign that at least some Feln appreciated that they were nothing like Steele and the humans who had stolen from them all those years ago. Even the guards looked much friendlier – now Zeina knew they weren't trying to kill them.

Eventually they reached a large archway leading into the mountain itself. It opened up into a cavernous chamber, where upon a stone table were food, drink, blankets, scarves, gloves and hats – anything they might need for their journey north.

'Rest and help yourselves!' trilled Hugrak. 'After you have eaten, there are rooms prepared for you to sleep.' He pointed towards the heart of the mountain down a stone corridor lit only by flickering torchlight. 'You will need your rest, in preparation for our journey tomorrow.'

Nedra headed directly to the hats, all knitted in bright colours and patterns, while Shrapnel and Sparks started trying on a selection of snow boots, lined in thick, woolly fur. Zeina went straight for the food, tucking into a big slice of pie covered in purple berries. It was absolutely delicious, and with all her nearest and dearest around her Zeina really began to feel like she was on holiday.

That was until she spotted the look on Jackson's face. He had sat across from her, his face as pale as snow, a newspaper gripped so tightly in his hands it looked as though he would rip it in two.

Zeina's fork, laden with crisp pastry and dark, juicy berries, froze in mid-air.

'What is it, Jackson?'

'See for yourself,' he choked.

He threw the paper to Zeina and collapsed on to the table, head in his hands.

THE SMOG SCOOP
Know the truth, trust the revolution

SINISTER STAN SYSTEM SOLD

Insider reports suggest that Hamilton Willoughby, head of the renowned Above family, has sold off one of his remaining assets in an attempt to fund his declining lifestyle. The STAN system, technology that takes complete control of a whale's motor system, had until recently made the Willoughbys the richest family in the four continents. But with fewer Aboves investing in whale hotels, that is beginning to change.

Our publication has been made aware of a deal, yet to be made public, which sold the rights of the patent and also much of the equipment from the STANS facility, where young whales were fitted with the abhorrent system, to an investor for a large sum. How long this will keep Hamilton Willoughby and his son Herbert in luxury is unknown. What is also unclear is what the investor, a new company called Osiris, wants with the technology or the equipment, much of which has now been removed from the facility. You can be sure our secret reporters will investigate further.

Pseudonym

'Oh, Jackson!' The article made Zeina's blood boil – she could only imagine how Jackson was feeling. Who was this company 'Osiris'? And what did they want with the patent and all the equipment from the STANS facility? No wild whales had been caught since Steele was killed so, as far as Zeina understood, the facility had been left unused.

'Have you seen this?' She held up the paper to her dad and

Parr, who broke off their conversation about supplies with Commander Hugrak and exchanged some rather guilty looks.

'How long have you known about it?' Jackson demanded furiously, grabbing the paper back to examine the date. 'Wait a minute, this issue is nearly A MONTH old!?'

The commander's hairy brows furrowed in confusion. 'I apologise. We in Palik love the *Smog Scoop* – indeed it's the only *human* newspaper we can bear. During the long winter it can take a while for the latest issues to make their way up here, but now it's spring we have more issues than we can read! I thought a collection of human newspapers might make you feel more at home, but I can see now it has caused upset.'

'Jackson, Zeina,' Captain Parr said firmly, glancing at Hugrak with a tight expression. 'We will discuss this *later*.'

'How could you keep this from me for a month?' Zeina glared at her dad, whose cheeks were flushed beneath his beard. He could look neither Zeina nor Jackson in the eye. 'Doesn't Jackson, at least, have the right to know?' Zeina looked around at her friends for support and realised in horror that it wasn't just her dad and Parr who were feeling guilty. 'Who else knew about this?'

Katu bowed his head in acknowledgement. Shrapnel blushed, folding his arms defensively across his chest. 'Look, it was captain's orders, Zee. I had no choice. That issue of the *Smog Scoop* was totally banned from the *Nightjar*. We weren't allowed to bring it on board or talk about it either.'

'Don't look at me! That's the first I've heard of it.' Nedra shrugged from the opposite end of the long table. 'I was busy being Lady Bellingham a month ago and there was nothing about the STAN system or Osiris in the *Ravenport Herald*!'

Sparks shrugged too; evidently she had also been left in the dark.

A painful tightness in her throat stopped Zeina from saying anything more. After everything that had happened to her last year, they were still treating her like a child. Hadn't it been she and Jackson who had stood up to Steele and saved the wild whale?

'It's not their fault, Zeina,' Jackson said, his voice as sharp as knives. 'They were just following orders. It's *hers*.' His eyes burned into Parr.

'Jackson, we will discuss this later,' she repeated firmly.

'NO,' he roared, making Zeina, Shrapnel and a number of the guards flinch in surprise. 'How could you keep this from me? We should return to the *Nightjar* at once! We need to go and find Hamilton *now*, before he can do any more damage. We must find this company – Osiris – before they can use the STANS technology on any new whales.'

'Jackson, Zeina.' Parr's voice was smaller now. She bent down to them, two red spots appearing uncharacteristically on her cheeks. 'I'm sorry I kept it from you. We are tackling this, I promise. But right now we are all needed here.'

'No,' Jackson replied sharply. 'You're captain of the Smog Rats – you have your own network of spies. You should have known about this before Pseudonym. You *promised* we would stop Hamilton before he could do any more harm. We have to investigate Osiris immediately. What do they want? Have you even found out where they have taken the equipment from the STANS facility?'

'Please, lad.' Parr was begging now. She looked nervously around at Hugrak and the rest of the guards, speaking in a whisper. 'Remember, Jackson, at the moment *nothing* is more important than this trip. I have Smog Rats out looking for Hamilton, I promise, and investigating Osiris. Once we are back, it's my first priority too. Please—'

The fingers of her mechanical hand closed into nothingness as Jackson brushed away her embrace and stormed off.

Zeina spent much of the rest of the evening in silence. She knew better than to go after Jackson. She had no words of comfort for him and knew he would prefer some time to calm down, alone. She scowled, watching her father and Parr loading provisions into backpacks, and Katu deep in conversation with Commander Hugrak around a large, unfolded map. She didn't feel like talking to any of the adults, nor to Shrapnel for that matter. He was ignoring her too – laughing and joking with Nedra as she tried on a tower of woolly hats.

'Don't you feel angry that they lied to us?' Zeina whispered to Sparks, who rolled her eyes.

'**THEY DIDN'T LIE**,' she wrote in her notebook. '**JUST DIDN'T SAY**.'

'That's the same thing!'

'**DIFFERENT**,' wrote Sparks, shaking her head. '**LIES ARE TRICKY BUT IF YOU LISTEN HARD ENOUGH PEOPLE ALWAYS GIVE AWAY THE THINGS THEY DON'T SAY**.'

Zeina thought carefully about this for a moment, before a rather curious idea entered her head.

'You might just be right, Sparks! Thanks!' she said, leaping to her feet. Hopefully the thought that had just occurred to her would be enough to get Jackson out of his mood.

The corridors carved into the mountain led to a series of round stone bedrooms, each just large enough for a Feln or two to curl up and sleep. These were all empty apart from the one she eventually found Jackson hiding in. He looked very small in the Feln-sized nest. A single torch, secured to a brace on the wall, illuminated his scrunched-up scowl peeping out from a pile of furry blankets he had wrapped himself in to keep warm.

'Leave me alone, Zeina,' he sulked.

Zeina ignored him and climbed up into his nest beside him, grabbing one of the blankets for her own shoulders.

'What if I told you I had a theory about who Pseudonym might be?' she whispered, eyes alight with mischief. It had the desired effect – his face un-scrunched.

'You do? How?'

'I think they might have just given themselves away,' Zeina smiled. 'When we were all looking at the *Scoop* – didn't you hear?'

Despite himself, Jackson's eyes filled with curiosity.

'Well, when I asked who knew about the article, did you hear what Nedra said?'

'She said she hadn't seen it because she was undercover as Lady Bellingham the week it came out.'

'Yes, *but* she also said, "There was nothing about Osiris in the *Ravenport Herald*." Remember?'

'So?' Jackson replied, exasperated. 'There wouldn't be! The *Smog Scoop* itself said the deal hadn't been made public. Only people who read that article would know about it.'

'Exactly!' Zeina grinned. 'She knew the name *Osiris*, but how? From where she was sitting today, right down the other end of the table, there's no way she could have read anything other than the headline and the headline didn't mention Osiris.'

Jackson looked unconvinced. 'Maybe she had read the article already but she didn't want to get involved after she saw how angry we both were with the others.'

'Could be, but Nedra doesn't seem to be someone who cares too much about what other people think of her. I think if she had heard of Osiris before, she would have said.'

'So,' Jackson replied, looking thoughtful, 'either she's lying about having read the article for some reason, or . . .'

'Or she wrote it herself!' Zeina exclaimed. 'Think about it, the *Smog Scoop* started up around the same time Nedra was freed from the mining grounds.'

Jackson's eyes lit up. 'She *is* a master of disguise. That would make it easy for her to find out information for the articles. If she's not Pseudonym, maybe she's the secret reporter?'

'Exactly!' Zeina was glad that her suspicions seemed to have done the trick. Jackson was already beginning to unfurl from the blankets he had cocooned himself in. 'Either way, it's definitely worth us investigating, isn't it? Just imagine the look on Parr's face if she's unknowingly invited Pseudonym along on a top-secret diplomacy mission!'

He smiled with delight. 'And if Nedra *is* Pseudonym, she'll have information about Hamilton. Perhaps she could tell us more about Osiris?'

'Maybe,' Zeina whispered, with less enthusiasm now.

There was something about the way Jackson looked whenever he spoke about Hamilton, something that was so far away from her gentle, caring Jackson. It unsettled her. Part of her hoped that investigating Nedra would distract him. Help him feel like he was doing *something*. 'So what do we do now?'

'We need proof. We'll need to catch her out somehow,' Jackson replied. 'If she's up here for the whole week, she's bound to try and write a story about it – Pseudonym wouldn't be able to resist!'

'She can't possibly run the whole thing alone,' Zeina continued. 'There must be printers and distributors, which means she'll have to send a raven to someone at some point. And if we can catch her out, she might even let us get involved with the *Scoop* in some way.'

Part of Zeina hoped that this might persuade Jackson to give up on his idea of joining the *Osprey* team. Jackson nodded, sitting up a little straighter.

'Parr would hate that,' he smiled, his steel-blue eyes twinkling. 'We could find out about what Osiris and Hamilton Willoughby are up to and share it with the world. That's more important than anything.'

'Exactly!' Zeina smiled.

CHAPTER 6

Their journey to the Glacial Palace began as soon as the sun had risen. Wrapped up in coats, scarves, gloves and snow boots, the party wound through the streets of Palik. Watching the cheerful town awaken in the gentle light of dawn almost made Jackson forget yesterday's fight with Parr.

He didn't enjoy feeling this angry all the time – he hated it, in fact – but his guardian had broken her promise. When he had agreed to join the Smog Rats rather than return to his old life, Captain Parr had promised they would find Hamilton and stop him. Six months on and not only was he still at large but now the STANS technology had been sold. It made Jackson shudder. What awful reason could Osiris have for buying it?

Just ahead of him was Nedra, a big green and gold hat pulled down over her ears. He watched as she chatted to Parr, and smiled to himself. Their captain would be furious if she found out she had inadvertently invited Pseudonym along on their secret mission!

Stone walkways were replaced by rocky mountain trails, which eventually weaved out on to a vast, deserted plain of white undulating peaks and troughs as far as the eye could see.

'The Glacial Palace is thirty miles north from here,' said Commander Hugrak.

'Thirty miles?!' spluttered Zeina, weighed down by her bulging backpack in which she had shoved the case containing her prototype. 'It will take *days* for us to travel thirty miles!'

The Feln commander laughed gruffly. 'It is not just you humans who have the ability to innovate, Zeina Starborn.'

And from underneath a sheet covered in a thick layer of snow, he revealed four strange vehicles. A cross between an airship and a sledge, each sat on three wide skis and possessed a large circular propeller at the back. In the middle was a wooden cocoon-shaped cockpit with two benches and a luggage rack.

Zeina's eyes danced as she stroked the strange snowmobiles.

'We call them Glindaskis,' Hugrak explained to Asher, who was equally entranced. 'Equal to anything you humans have designed, I'm sure you'd agree?'

'Powered by wind?' Asher asked, examining the steel cage that contained the mighty propeller in wonder.

'Mostly,' replied Hugrak. 'They just need a little bit of *this* to get them going.' He popped a small square of white into a little chamber and set it alight. It sparked and then flamed, releasing a rather unpleasant smell that Jackson found strangely familiar. The propeller leapt into life. Hugrak went from one machine to the next and soon the quiet ice plain was filled with the sound of whirring propellers. Zeina sniffed the air, her nose crinkling as if she too was trying to place the smell. But there was no time for Jackson to ask. Hugrak was shouting over the noise and ushering people towards the machines. 'Come, come – no time to wait around! You can meet the Glindaski's brilliant innovator once we reach the palace.'

'Nedra! Come on – get in with us!' Zeina called over, elbowing Jackson into the nearest vehicle. She rose an eyebrow as Nedra agreed, slipping in next to one of the Feln guards in the driving seat, while Zeina and Jackson wedged themselves on to the bench behind. Shrapnel and Sparks got into a second Glindaski with another guard, Parr and Asher a third, leaving Katu and Commander Hugrak at the very front of the procession.

'Strap in,' smiled the driver, and Jackson barely had time to click his lap-belt in place before the machine thrust forward at an almighty speed. The landscape whipped past them, a blur of white and blue. Jackson pulled down his hat to protect his ears from the sting of the freezing air.

'Here,' called Nedra from the front, passing Jackson and Zeina a blanket from her footwell. 'Bit chilly, isn't it?' she laughed.

'Have you been to the Northern Continent before?' Zeina shouted over the noise of the rushing landscape.

'Me? Never!' Nedra exclaimed. 'I grew up on the Eastern Continent, but I was in the mining grounds by the time I was ten.'

Zeina gave Jackson a swift nudge under their blanket.

'You got out just a few months ago, didn't you? How did you escape?' he said, uncertain of really what to ask.

'Oh, no one escapes from the mining grounds.' Her usually cheerful smile clouded over. 'The only way out is to work out your sentence, but many die before that can happen. Sometimes a family member can buy you out – bribe a guard – but for that you need to have family.' Her eyes glazed over. 'I was liberated with the rest of my ore mine by the Kotarth army as they claimed back their lands. I've been out four months next week.'

'How long were you there?' asked Zeina.

'You lose track,' she replied, her face becoming grey and haunted. 'About six years in total.'

'Six years? All alone, at ten years old?' Jackson exclaimed, his heart breaking for her.

'Well, not all alone, not for all of the time. My mother, she . . .' Nedra drifted off and then shook her head, as if trying

66

to shake off the memory. 'Listen, do you mind if we talk about something else?'

'Of course, I'm so sorry,' said Zeina, her own eyes becoming misty. 'How do you like spying for the Smog Rats?'

'I really do love it. As a kid, before I was arrested, I used to love dressing up. I never had much, you see, so I used to scavenge for things the Aboves threw away and do a bit of pickpocketing, jewels mainly. That's what got me arrested in the end.' Zeina leaned forward and squeezed her hand, and the two looked into each other's eyes, a shared understanding that Jackson could never be a part of – growing up he had never needed to steal or scavenge for anything.

'Anyway, in the mining grounds I spent hours and hours imagining, pretending I was someone else in my head, and that's basically all spying is,' Nedra continued. 'The jewels are a bonus, of course.' She winked, reaching inside her coat to pull out a brooch with a large purple stone cut into the shape of a whale. 'The pickpocketing is much better now I'm hobnobbing with the great and the good on the sky whale hotels!'

The brooch shone from the centre of Nedra's palm and Jackson saw Zeina's eyes light up as she reached out to touch it.

'Go on!' Nedra laughed. 'You can have that one if you like, Zeina. I've got another!' She pulled a brooch from her pocket – this one was a glimmering ruby, also cut into the shape of a whale. 'I've checked and they're just made of glass, not worth a bean, but they are very pretty.'

Jackson watched as Zeina took the brooch and fastened it to the collar of her coat. She beamed proudly.

'I'll find one for you, Jackson, on my next trip. Something like a sapphire would really bring out your eyes!'

Nedra laughed, turning back to the magnificent view in front of them.

It occurred to Jackson that if Nedra *was* Pseudonym, catching her out may not be as easy as they had first thought. She was a *spy*, after all, a professional teller of lies. Unless Nedra slipped up again, it was going to be tricky.

A commotion up ahead drew Jackson from his thoughts as their Glindaski slowed right down, skidding to a stop behind the other three. Katu and Commander Hugrak had got out to inspect the ice plain ahead, which ended abruptly in a deep crack, splitting the landscape in two. The gap was at least two metres across and rose on the opposite side in a giant cliff of blue ice. The noise of the propellers was replaced by the sound of water gushing somewhere far below and the voices of Katu and Hugrak arguing.

'It isn't safe,' Katu grumbled. 'It's far too early.'

'Come now, cousin,' Hugrak laughed. 'You worry too much. We are used to the conditions changing – every year is slightly different. We must just travel around.'

A grumble from the cliff sent a ledge of ice crashing into the crevasse.

'It is unstable!' gestured Katu. 'And if there are fissures this wide and this deep, there are bound to be smaller ones covered completely by snowfall. We wouldn't know about them until one of us fell in.'

'What's going on?' asked Parr, climbing out of her vehicle.

'The ice plains are changing all the time, Captain,' said Hugrak. 'Your friend here worries far too much! It will make the journey an hour longer maybe, but we can go round. We'll still make it to the palace before sundown.'

'That is the sound of the ice plain melting,' explained Katu, his tail swishing in irritation. 'A waterfall of melted ice forming a lake somewhere beneath the ice. This ice plain is not safe. We should turn around.'

Hugrak's jovial tone became sharp as he rose to his full height. 'And whose land is this?' he growled. 'Who here knows best what is *safe*? You must think either I wish to endanger my king's guests or that I am a complete idiot. Which is it?'

Parr stepped between the two beings. 'Commander Hugrak, are you confident that if we continue you can find a safe route that will get us to the palace before the sun goes down?'

'Of course!' he scoffed. 'I know this land as well as the pads of my paw.'

'Captain Parr,' Katu snarled. 'A crevasse of this size wouldn't usually be found this far north and certainly not this early in the season. Here, look, there are man-sized holes too. If he cannot see how dangerous—'

Hugrak roared, swiping the air above Katu's head with one great clawed paw.

'Stop it, both of you!' Parr braced herself, both arms, human and mechanical, outstretched to keep them apart.

A loud caw from above made them all freeze. Instead of rushing to Katu's aid, the bird hovered above the scene, squawking angrily up into the sky. Jackson spotted it first, the unmistakeable shadow of an Upper Atmosphere airship breaking through the shifting snow clouds, followed by the clanking of pistons and whirring of giant propellers.

'Quick!' roared Hugrak, his fight with Katu quite forgotten. 'Guards, get the Glindaskis behind that peak. The rest of you, down here.'

He led the way down behind a peak of snow and ice near the edge of the crevasse. There was a hole melted in the centre, just large enough for him to squeeze his large frame down and into a hollow cavern of ice below.

One by one, they gripped Hugrak's great paw and let him guide them down into the cavern. It opened on one side into the crevasse itself, nothing but a small ledge of ice stopping them from falling into the abyss of darkness below. The great cliff face of the opposite side stretched up into the sky.

Jackson flattened himself against the frozen wall, holding his breath as the airship passed over the narrow chink of sky above them. The sound grew and then faded, eerily mechanical against the natural sound of the waterfall. Just when Jackson thought he could begin to relax, there was a grumble from the ice cliff opposite. Another enormous ledge slid down the cliff face, crashing against the ledge and missing Nedra by mere centimetres. She stifled a scream.

'Whoa, that was too close,' whispered Shrapnel. 'Come on, the airship has gone. Let's get out of here before it's too late.'

Hugrak agreed, gesturing for the group to start filing back along the ledge towards the cavern's opening. Jackson was stopped by Zeina, frozen to the spot on the ledge, staring wide-eyed at the cliff face where the ledge had fallen. She gripped his arm.

'Jackson, what in the world is THAT?'

CHAPTER 7

One by one the whole party froze, each staring in amazement at the wall of ice in front of them. Suspended within the ice-bound cliff were the skull and bones of a colossal horned beast – a tapered spine, opening into a cavernous rib cage, shortened arm bones with long fingers splayed out like a fan, a great, yawning jawbone, complete with short, sharp teeth and then, protruding from the very tip of the skull, two enormous spiralling tusks.

'What *is* it?' asked Zeina, mesmerised.

'The skeleton of a horned sky whale,' Katu answered, 'frozen in time within the ice plain.'

Zeina studied it. Without its skin and blubber, she hadn't been sure what type of creature it was at all. But now she noticed the distinct whale-like shape, the front limbs fanned out like flippers and the fact there were no back limbs at all.

'I didn't even know there were *horned* sky whales,' said Jackson.

'They are very shy creatures,' Katu replied. 'Human sightings have been limited to just a handful in recent years, so few that they have entered the realm of myths.'

Zeina's dad laughed. 'You won't remember, Zeina, but your mum used to sing you a song about a whale with twin twisted tusks when you were small. I thought they were just stories.'

Zeina closed her eyes, as she always did when her dad spoke of her mum, desperately trying to recapture the memory. Nothing came.

'Was it a baby whale?' she asked sadly, for despite its huge size it was much smaller than the young sky whale they rescued last year.

'No, by the size of those tusks it was definitely an adult when it died. Horned sky whales are a much smaller species than the sky whales humans use for their whale hotels,' said Katu.

'How many species of sky whale are there?' Shrapnel asked.

'Many,' Katu replied. 'Thankfully most of them learned long ago to stay away from the parts of our world inhabited by humans.'

'The horned sky whales are protected by the Feln,' Hugrak explained gruffly. 'After Steele's airship came to steal our ancestral treasure, we signed an agreement with humans – no

73

airships north of Palik. That was to protect the horned sky whales as much as us.'

'Which is what makes that airship we saw even more worrying,' Katu growled.

'Yes,' Hugrak agreed begrudgingly. 'We must get to the Glacial Palace quickly. I need to inform the king.'

A rumble somewhere nearby, followed by a crash, signalled that another part of the cliff face had broken off and fallen down into the fissure below.

'Come on,' Captain Parr said. 'Let's get out of here before anything else happens. You're still confident you can get us there before dusk, Commander?'

'Certainly, Captain Parr,' he replied, pushing them one by one up through the roof of the cavern and out on to the surface of the plain.

It was nearing sundown by the time they first spotted the Glacial Palace, an eerie silhouette against a flaming sky. The palace cast long shadows across the ice plain, dark fingers that seemed to beckon them towards it. It was only as the Glindaskis drew to a stop outside the entrance that Zeina could appreciate the palace's full scale. Giant ice bricks, each the height of a human, were built into a large circular hall and covered by a domed roof made from compacted snow. Arc-shaped entrance doors had been sculpted to each show half of a Feln king, his eyes and sun-shaped crown glowing emerald from real jewels set into the ice. From this central hall sprawled a network of smaller ice domes and towers, all decorated with intricate ice sculptures. A spiral tower of frozen steps formed the tallest point of the palace and at the very pinnacle an enormous green crystal glowed like an eye.

'All *this* is made new every year?' asked Zeina, staring up at a large ice warrior holding aloft a giant icy sun. On the other side of the doors, Jackson inspected an identical warrior, this one holding a moon.

'That's right,' said Hugrak, loading himself with bags and provisions. 'The palace is remade every winter from the ice of the Kalder River, but its design and location change each year. It takes several weeks to build and won't start to melt until the end of the month of Valco Sol. After the Equinox celebrations the king returns to his mountain palace, and by the time summer comes it will look as though nothing were ever here. You are very lucky, all of you,' he pointed at Shrapnel, Sparks and Nedra, who were examining another sculpture, this one a large horned sky whale sailing between a sun and a moon, 'to be among the few humans in the entire world who have ever seen the wonders of a Feln ice palace.'

The palace's interior was every bit as grand as its exterior. Zeina examined the enormous chandelier that shimmered from the roof of the entrance hall – each icy crystal carved by hand, Commander Hugrak told them. Although she could not imagine wanting to take off her woolly hat or gloves anytime soon, it felt warm in comparison to the biting cold outside. Hugrak rushed off to tell the king of their arrival, and servants in green and gold tailcoats led the group down a long corridor, flanked by glimmering spiral ice pillars.

Their sleeping quarters were surprisingly cosy. Down narrow tunnels, they each had their own individual little snow dome, lined with furry blankets. Zeina made sure she and Jackson claimed ones right next to Nedra, so they could keep an eye on her.

There was no space in their beds for their packs and belongings, but there was an area outside with a stove, benches, cupboards and pegs. One of the servants offered to take Zeina's case containing her prototype to the workshop so it could be locked up for the night and, terrified her dad might ask to examine it if she left it in the communal area, Zeina agreed. At one end was a small ice window to the outside, although it was so dark now, they could see little through it.

'Would your ice raven like to join the king's in the royal aviary?' a servant asked Katu, gesturing to a larger snow dome filled with the beautiful white birds. They squawked and cawed, preening themselves and feeding from a large bowl filled with fish, upon a giant icy pedestal. Every now and then, one would disappear through a chute in the ceiling, transforming, as ice ravens do, into a diamond flash.

'He's not *my* ice raven,' grumbled Katu. 'Although if there's food, I should think he would indeed.'

And without so much as a backward squawk, Albi flew off to join his fellows perching around the icy bowl.

The dining room was grander still than the entrance hall. Around a long, frozen table were twenty dining chairs, their tall backs each carved into a different design. Zeina grabbed one topped with a miniature ice palace, Jackson – a deer with antlers, Sparks – a leaping fish. There were sky whales, suns, ice ravens, moons and stars. The most impressive of all was the throne at the head of the table, which was carved into a magnificent Feln king with a diamond crown and twin jewelled staffs. Behind the throne, two curved ice staircases led up to a balcony that stretched the full length of the room, presumably so that someone could light the candles in all five of the spectacular frozen chandeliers.

Captain Parr stood behind the chair nearest the throne and motioned for everyone to remain standing. There was the sound of a horn, before a procession of Feln entered – two guards, followed by Commander Hugrak and then a number of Feln wearing richly embroidered capes, waistcoats and fur-lined jackets, all decorated in gold. Finally, flanked on all sides by servants and guards, was the Emerald King himself – one of the most magnificent beings Zeina had ever seen.

He wore a thick, green cape, ornate with golden needlework and emerald beads, and so long that it brushed against the icy floor. Two servants rushed forward to assist him as he approached the table, one to take from him a white spiral staff and the other to hold the end of his cape. There was silence as his large frame filled the impressive throne, giant paws resting atop the ones made of ice. On his head rested a gold crown, fur-lined and glittering with giant emeralds. He smiled, showing off a set of enormous pointed canines.

'Please, sit,' he said, his voice a powerful snarl.

The Feln guests took up their places behind their dining chairs and all bowed low before sitting down. Captain Parr bowed too, signalling for the rest of them to do the same. Zeina did as she was told but couldn't help feeling a little bit ridiculous being so formal when they still all had their woolly hats, gloves and coats on. Nedra caught Zeina's eye across the table and gave her a wink.

'Welcome, honoured guests!' the king boomed. 'Dinner is served.'

In strode an army of servants carrying all manner of dishes. There were stews and sliced meats, purple pickles and pies, and a whole fish covered in a sticky berry sauce.

78

'Please excuse our dress,' Captain Parr said to the king. 'We are not so well adapted as the Feln to these temperatures.'

'My grand palace isn't warm enough for you?' the king roared, baring his teeth.

'Oh, that's not what I—' replied Parr.

But the king erupted into hearty, growling laughter.

'Don't worry, Captain. I know you humans are poorly adapted to our lands.' His eyes glinted as he licked purple juice from his jaws.

'That is sadly true, King.'

'"Emerald King" is the title I prefer, Captain Parr, now that the Emerald Crown is back where it belongs.' He lifted his furry chin proudly, making the dark-green jewels sparkle in the light.

'That crown was part of the treasure acquired by Vivianne Steele, was it not, Emerald King?' asked Katu.

There was a hush around the table – the sounds of chatter and claws against plates stopped as the assembled Feln stared in horror at Katu.

'We do not mention that name here, Prince Katu,' growled the king. 'This crown was *stolen* from my father. And now that awful human is dead, it is my greatest honour to have been able to return our sacred Emerald Crown to its home. You were her employee, were you not?' he added, black crescent-shaped pupils narrowing on Katu.

'Katu has served the Smog Rats for many years now, Emerald King,' Captain Parr interrupted, before Katu could answer. Zeina was sure she had felt Parr give him a swift kick under the table. 'The Kotarth share in our objectives, and we support them reclaiming their stolen lands in the west.'

'Yes, yes. There will be time for all this talk of politics tomorrow.' The king waved his paw and then focused back on his food, picking up a large chunk of fish in his claws. He munched it in his powerful jaws, licking the dark sticky sauce from his beard afterwards. 'Tell me, where are the Starborns? It is thanks to them that any of you are here at all. My innovator, Lotti Grenn, insisted.' The king gestured to the Feln across from Zeina. 'She invented those rather remarkable Glindaskis that got you here safely.'

Zeina smiled at Lotti, who was slightly smaller than the other Feln. Her fur was smoky grey rather than white, and dappled all over with black rosettes. Her grey eyes gleamed intently.

'I have followed news of your remarkable innovations, Starborns,' she nodded. 'And now I hear you are inventing solar-powered technology?'

'That's right,' replied Zeina's dad. 'This is my daughter, Zeina. She has been working on the prototype, which should be ready in the next couple of days. We would be honoured to give you a demonstration, Emerald King.' He placed one hand proudly on Zeina's shoulder in a way she wished he wouldn't.

'Both the Emerald King and I value the natural world above all else,' Lotti purred. 'We know that the future relies on finding renewable technology.'

The king grunted, tearing the head off a fish and licking the meat from its spine.

'Your Glindaskis are truly remarkable,' Zeina's dad commended. 'Mainly powered by the wind, I gather?'

'Yes! They just need a little bit of fuel to get them going – we use a few square centimetres of dried whale blubber, which on a normal winter's day will keep them going for many hours. Very economical.'

Something dawned on Zeina, and one look at Jackson made it clear that he too had also just remembered why the smell of the Glindaskis seemed so familiar. The last time they had smelled it was on Steele's ship, the *Raven*. It was the same smell that had seeped from the walls of their cabins on the old whaling ship whenever they passed over the furnaces of the mining grounds.

'You burn *sky whale* blubber?' Jackson asked, his brows furrowed.

'Yes, and eat whale meat and make jewellery from their tusks.' The king gestured for his servant to bring him his staff.

He twirled it proudly in his paws and now Zeina could see that it was not made of ice at all. The spiral staff, covered in patterns and set with jewels, was in fact the carved tusk of a horned sky whale.

'I thought you *protected* the whales?' Zeina asked, a little more harshly than it had sounded in her head. Captain Parr's eye found Zeina's and frowned.

'We do!' the king growled, guzzling purple liquid from a white chalice.

'Once a year, we take just one horned sky whale,' Lotti explained. 'One older whale, near the end of its natural life. We use the blubber, meat, bones and tusks. Nothing is wasted. The blubber is dried and used for fuel, the meat is preserved and will last the entire population of Palik City the whole of the way through winter. Bones and tusks make our plates, drinking cups and weapons.'

'Without that and our lilaberries, the Feln wouldn't make it through the winter,' the king said, raising his chalice. 'You could not imagine how beautiful the mountainsides look in summer, purple and plump with delicious lilaberries. They make glorious wine too!'

Zeina felt torn. After the horror of watching Steele and her crew capture the baby sky whale last year, the thought of the Feln catching a horned sky whale to cut up and eat made her feel uncomfortable. She wanted to ask more about how they hunted them, but one look at Parr made it clear that now was not the time.

'Will we get to see any horned sky whales while we are here?' Shrapnel asked.

'Yes, of course,' Commander Hugrak answered. 'They begin to reappear in this region with the return of the sun—'

'I must ask you, Emerald King, what are you planning to do about the airship we spotted?' Katu interrupted rudely, making Parr glare at him across the table. 'To protect the horned sky whales properly, there must be no human airships north of Palik.'

'You worry too much, cousin,' the king replied, placing one of his great white paws over Katu's. 'Commander Hugrak told me about the ship. It is *nothing* to worry about. Every year we get a few tourists coming a little further north than they should, dreaming of a glimpse of our magnificent Glacial Palace. The weather always gets to them eventually. They'll not find us or the whales.'

'I must disagree—' Katu started, his tail beginning to swish behind his icy chair.

'Ha!' the king laughed, although his eyes glinted with malice. 'You disagree with the Emerald King?'

Zeina found it odd that the king kept referring to himself by his title, but she wouldn't dare let her amusement show – clearly it meant an awful lot to him.

83

'I do,' replied Katu. 'The airship should be investigated, as should the thickness and condition of the ice plain. Temperatures here are not cold enough for this time of year.'

The fearsome king erupted into big, booming howls of laughter, but Zeina noticed the fur on his neck beginning to stand on end and a new tension in his claws that scratched deep grooves into the frozen table. 'Not cold enough! Look at your friends.' He gestured to the humans round the table, still all wrapped up in their winter clothes.

Katu opened his mouth as if to argue but anything he was about to say was cut off by Parr banging her cup on the table.

'I think that's *enough*, Katu,' she said through gritted teeth, glaring at him fiercely.

A servant came in and whispered something to the king.

'Ah, honoured guests, we have a surprise for you,' he smiled. 'Please, follow me.' He rose, servants hurrying to adjust his cloak as he strode towards the arched doorway between the staircases.

Through the doorway was a large circular room. There were no chandeliers or ice lamps in here, but the room was brightly moonlit by a skylight, a giant pane of ice that covered the whole of the roof. Looking up made Zeina feel small and strange – the endless sky, glittering with stars, was the most beautiful she had ever seen and yet she could not help but wonder how the window was held up. Surely if it fell it would crush them all to death.

The king chuckled while all around him the Smog Rats 'ooohhed' and 'aaahhed', captivated by the view. The sky seemed to shimmer and dance, rivers of greens and turquoise against the dark midnight blue.

'We call it Smara Ignis,' the king explained. 'But you might better understand the name "Emerald Fire", a beautiful trail the sun leaves behind to get us through the last of the long, dark nights. It is said that our magnificent emeralds hold the spirit of Smara Ignis within them and it is true; since the return of the Emerald Crown, the sky fire has burned with a renewed intensity. A show of how powerful the Feln will become under my reign.'

'Look, there!' cried Nedra, pointing up towards a small shadow, dark against the green light. 'Is that . . . ?'

Zeina followed Nedra's gaze, lit with wonder, and spotted it – the silhouette of a small whale with twin twisted tusks.

That morning she hadn't even known such a beast existed and now she was seeing it – albeit from a distance – in real life!

'Ah, yes,' the king replied. 'A horned sky whale – but we shall do our best to get you a better view before you leave.'

CHAPTER 8

J ackson was awoken by the echoes of hushed voices drifting down into his snow dome. All curled up in cosy blankets, he had been surprisingly snug during the night and it took him a few moments to work out exactly where he was and who the voices belonged to.

'I shouldn't have to remind you how important the king's support is, Katu. You're meant to be here to help build a relationship,' whispered Parr.

'The king is up to something, I'm sure of it,' Katu answered. 'Either he truly doesn't understand the significance of the situation, or there is something he is hiding.'

'Even if he is, he won't respond to threats or to you questioning his every move. *Please* can you try to hold your tongue today,' Parr implored. 'Once he signs an alliance, *then* you can challenge him as you see fit. But right now we need him on side.'

'As you wish . . .'

Their voices faded with the sounds of their snow boots on the frozen floor.

Despite how furious he was with Parr for concealing that issue of the *Scoop*, Jackson couldn't help but feel a little sorry for her. Last night's royal dinner had not gone well – Katu and the Emerald King seemed to disagree on many things. Despite Parr's pleading, Jackson could not imagine stubborn Katu letting the king off that easily.

A muffled creaking signified that someone nearby was pushing down the narrow snow tunnel from their sleeping quarters.

Jackson gathered all his strength to leave behind his cosy hollow and ease himself down his own tunnel, just in time to see a pair of snow boots creep past the opening. Craning his head so that only his eyes peeped out, he saw the back of someone disappear in a flash around the corner towards the aviary. Why were they in such a hurry? Could it be Nedra – off to send a raven perhaps?

Although he wasn't certain that she *was* Pseudonym, he was enjoying the chase; the mystery was a welcome distraction from his rage. He felt sure Pseudonym would have information about Hamilton's whereabouts, and after months of stewing it felt good to be doing something positive towards catching him again.

He clambered out of his tunnel as quickly as he could and stuck his head down the one that led to Zeina's sleeping chamber.

'Zeina!' he said as quietly as he could. '*Zeina*,' he repeated a little more loudly, for she was known to be a heavy sleeper.

'WAH?' Zeina jumped awake, all twisted in her blankets, her woolly hat askew. She blinked, blurry-eyed. 'Jackson? What is it?'

'I think it might be Nedra,' he whispered. 'Someone's up already and visiting the aviary!'

This snapped Zeina out of her slumber and within seconds they were both standing in the area outside their sleeping chambers. But no sooner had she grabbed his arm than they were interrupted by Asher.

'Morning! Where are you two off in such a hurry?' he said, his head and chest protruding out of his tunnel. 'Zeina, it's a quick breakfast for you this morning and then we're going straight to Lotti's workshop to finish the solar tech. You heard how interested the king was last night at dinner.'

Jackson noticed Zeina's face fall, their pursuit of Nedra quite forgotten.

'You don't have to come, Dad,' she said. 'I want to finish it myself.'

'Nonsense! After Katu's performance last night, impressing the king with our solar tech could be the key to an alliance. Parr needs all the help she can get.'

As if they had heard them, Parr and Katu appeared from the corridor, followed by Shrapnel, who was already wrapped up in his outdoor gear and carrying an enormous pile of delicious-looking pastries, topped with lilaberry jam.

'These are *amazing*,' Shrapnel managed between mouthfuls, handing them out to Zeina and Jackson. Sparks appeared and he gave one to her too. She grinned, licking sticky jam from her fingers before giving them a thumbs up.

'Where's Nedra?' Parr asked, frowning as she examined her pocket watch.

'I wouldn't worry about Ned, Captain,' Shrapnel replied, wiping the last crumbs of his breakfast from his face. 'She's always wandering off. She'll have gone outside for a bit. She hates being cooped up inside after all those years in the mining grounds. She's used to looking after herself.'

'That's understandable, but we all have an appointment with the king this morning and it won't do to be late.'

'Here I am, Captain,' Nedra said, panting slightly as she hurried down the corridor. She had her green and gold hat pulled down over her ears and a few fresh snowflakes dappled her nose and cheeks. If these were from a trip to the aviary, she did not look in the least bit flustered. 'It's a beautiful morning,' she smiled. 'The sunrises here are spectacular.'

'Right, now we're all here.' Parr ushered them towards her. 'The plan for today is as follows: this morning we have all been invited on a tour of the Glacial Palace by the king himself. I'm sure I don't need to remind any of you to be

89

polite and appreciative. I know you will all be your delightfully charming selves. With no talk of politics. Is that clear?'

She glared around at her crew, her gaze lingering on Katu most of all. They all nodded.

'After lunch, the Starborns will head to Lotti's workshop to put the finishing touches to the solar tech. Katu and I will have a meeting with the king, and the rest of you have been invited to race the Glindaskis with Commander Hugrak.'

There were instant celebrations from Shrapnel, Sparks and Nedra. Zeina turned crimson.

'Do you think it wise to leave the children unaccompanied with Commander Hugrak?' Katu grumbled. 'Especially outside on the ice plain.'

Nedra and Shrapnel both opened their mouths to protest.

'Dad should go!' Zeina gabbled. 'I'm sure I'll be able to finish the solar tech with some help from Lotti. Go on, Dad, you would love to see what the Glindaskis can really do.'

'You understand the importance of the tech, Zeina?' Parr frowned. 'It *is* nearly finished?'

'Of course!' Zeina replied, her eyes unnaturally bright.

'Humm.' Her father stroked his beard. 'And I can come and examine it later today?'

Zeina nodded vigorously. Jackson rolled his eyes, always surprised at the number of times – through sheer cheek – that Zeina got her own way. It was an attribute that had irritated him enormously in the first few weeks of their friendship; now it was something he rather admired.

'Great. That's settled then.' Parr smiled. 'We'll meet back in the dining room for afternoon tea at dusk.'

The Glacial Palace was larger than Jackson had imagined – a maze of corridors and galleries, each beautifully decorated, ready for the Equinox celebrations. The Emerald King, escorted everywhere by two guards and a whole group of servants, showed them around his throne room, drawing room, the ballroom and the banqueting hall, which had ten ice tables, each the size of the one they had dined at the night before. Every minute detail, from the clawed feet of his magnificent throne to each pendant dangling from the five ballroom chandeliers, was constructed completely from snow and ice. Jackson kept a close eye on Nedra, but if she was trying to sneak away, it was not at all obvious. She seemed just as enraptured as the rest of them.

The king was much more interested in showing off his magnificent palace than talking about sky whales or the Smog Rats' cause. In fact, whenever Parr tried to guide him on to such topics, he would simply change the subject or stop the group to point out a particularly beautiful ice carving or sculpture.

It was the king's treasury that fascinated Jackson most of all. Frozen completely within great slabs of ice were axes, spears, swords and catapults, made either in glittering gold or iridescent sky whale tusk and set with precious stones. There were crowns, rings, belts and collars, each encrusted with jewels.

The children all crowded around a ruby suspended within a case of ice. Easily the size of Jackson's head, its brilliant red glow illuminated their wonderstruck faces.

'What do you make of that then, Ned?' Shrapnel whispered. 'Think you could fit it in your pocket?'

Nedra laughed. 'That's beyond even my talents, I think.'

'Well, now.' The king glided towards them. 'If it is *gems* that interest you, I have something of *far* greater value. For the king of all jewels is the *emerald* and I have the largest in the four continents – the famous Emerald Crystal.'

The king led them up a staircase that spiralled above the domed roof of the treasury and out into the biting wind. Higher and higher, they corkscrewed above the gleaming white palace. Jackson glimpsed down but instantly wished he hadn't – there was no handrail at all, nothing to stop them falling to their deaths if they slipped on the icy steps. He pulled his coat around him and tried to keep as close to the curved inner wall as possible.

At the very top of the staircase was a circular platform and raised above it, set upon giant ice prongs, was the largest jewel Jackson had ever seen. Deep green and glowing with a smoky mystery, it seemed to hold stories and secrets. They all stood completely mesmerised for a second.

'Beautiful, isn't it?' The Emerald King smiled proudly. 'My Feln ancestors mined this stone from our mountains over a thousand years ago and it has been a tradition to use it as the centrepiece for our Glacial Palace ever since. We believe it strengthens the spirit of the Smara Ignis. The bright trails in our skies are seen as a good omen to get us through our harsh winters.'

'Quite captivating, Emerald King,' Katu remarked with a flick of his ears. 'But, forgive me, the Emerald Crystal was also part of the treasure plundered by Steele, I believe?'

'It was, cousin,' the king replied frostily. 'The decades when both the crown and the crystal were in that woman's possession were a great source of misery for the Feln. I'm proud that it is I who have returned them to their proper place. And, indeed, this year has seen the brightest Emerald Fire in a generation, something that has brought great joy to my subjects.'

'There were rumours Steele had hidden them in a secret vault located somewhere in the mining grounds, weren't there?' Katu pushed.

'Why should I know, or care, about where *humans* keep their plunder?' the king growled. 'What matters now is that they are back where they belong.'

Katu stroked his beard slowly, his whiskers twitching. 'Of course, Emerald King. I just wondered how you managed to reclaim them so soon after Steele's death.'

'Since her demise, her followers have been falling over themselves to sell her treasure.' The king laughed. 'Nothing shakes a human's loyalty like gold!'

'I agree, the greed of some is astonishing,' smiled Katu. 'How ever did you manage to raise enough money to buy back such priceless items?'

Parr shot Katu a withering stare.

'You are impertinent, Prince Katu,' the king growled. 'The treasure is back where it belongs and Steele is dead. That's all that matters.'

'But those like her are not, Emerald King,' said Asher gently. 'There's ore in your Northern Mountains too. Those that need it will come here.'

'If we do nothing to stop them, the Aboves will completely destroy the Northern and Western Continents, just as they have the south. Both of our kind are in danger of being wiped out, like the Zugmi,' Katu pronounced.

'But for now *my* subjects, at least, are safe,' the king snarled.

'I must disagree, Emerald King. We saw that airship for ourselves on our journey from Palik.'

'And I have told you, Prince Katu, that is none of your concern!' the king roared, rising up to his full height, his jaws

94

just centimetres from Katu's head. Zeina rushed to his side, grabbing Katu's paw. For a moment Jackson worried that the king would knock them both from the tower with one swipe, and yet Zeina's presence seemed to shake the king from his wild anger.

'Enough,' he growled loudly. 'Enough of this, now! It is time for lunch.' And he marched down the perilous steps, his gaggle of servants bustling after him.

An uneasy silence descended on the group over lunch; the only sounds came from the king as he chomped on fish after fish and washed it all down with great mouthfuls of lilaberry wine. It was after they had all had their fill, after Commander Hugrak had come to escort them to the Glindaskis, after they had dropped Zeina off at Lotti's workshop on the way, that Jackson noticed Nedra was missing for the second time that day.

She must have sloped off somewhere between Lotti's workshop and reaching the shelter outside the palace where the Glindaskis were kept. Jackson could remember her standing next to Asher as he reminded Zeina that he'd be back to inspect the finished solar tech after dinner. But by the time they were all piling into the Glindaskis, she was gone.

'Where's Nedra?' Jackson asked Sparks, who looked tiny squashed up next to the enormous Commander Hugrak.

'**FORGOT HER SCARF**,' Sparks wrote on her pad.

Jackson frowned, desperately trying to remember whether Nedra was wearing her scarf when they left the dining room.

'What did I tell you? Ned's always disappearing!' Shrapnel shouted over the whirring propellers. 'You can be my co-pilot until she gets back, Asher.'

'I've barely recovered from the last time you were *my* co-pilot,' Asher laughed, grabbing the wrist he injured when he and Shrapnel crashed their airship in the Western Mountains the year before. But he clambered in next to him all the same.

Jackson began backing away from the Glindaski. If Nedra was indeed Pseudonym, this could be his chance to catch her out. 'I'll just go and see if—'

'Get in, boy,' Hugrak said in a deep, commanding growl. 'I've been given the task of entertaining you this afternoon and there'll be no more wandering off.'

The commander's snarl, his flinty glare and the way Sparks's large eyes pleaded with Jackson made it very difficult to argue otherwise.

CHAPTER 9

Zeina couldn't help but feel a little hard done by; she would have much preferred to be racing Glindaskis than working on her solar tech. But at least her dad had been persuaded to stay away, for now. She needed to get it finished so she could concentrate on investigating whether Nedra was Pseudonym.

Lotti grinned as Zeina entered the workshop, lifting up a pair of magnified goggles and putting down the tools she was using to tinker with a piece of machinery.

'Zeina, welcome!'

The workshop reminded Zeina of her dad's back in Ravenport – a semi-organised mess of tools, scraps of paper covered with doodles, and all manner of half-constructed things. The only differences were that this workshop was at least triple the size and Lotti had an enormous ice window that gave her a magnificent view of the sun above the mountains.

'Amazing,' Zeina said, her eyes wide with wonder.

'Isn't it?' smiled Lotti, passing her a tool belt and a leather apron. 'Here. I haven't peeked, I promise, but I can't wait to see it!'

Lotti pushed Zeina's case containing her prototype towards her and a knot twisted in Zeina's stomach. She had no choice but to come clean.

'Listen, it's not quite as finished as I would have hoped. I mean . . . I know I *can* finish it . . . It's just . . .'

Lotti laughed, though not unkindly. 'You sound just like me when I've promised the king I'm on the edge of a breakthrough. Just show me. It's probably not as bad as you think.'

Zeina found her keys, opened up her case and got out her things – a web of wires connected a small lightbulb to her prototype solar unit. The base was black sandstone from the Southern Continent with a layer of titanium, hammered flat, from the frames of discarded velocycles. The top was the glass from a quartz magnifying glass. Zeina covered it with black cloth as she set everything up on a workbench near the great window.

With a nervous breath, she put on a pair of safety goggles and waited for Lotti to do the same.

Zeina whisked the black cloth away and sunlight hit the quartz, making it glisten. For at least three seconds, Zeina thought that this time it had worked – the bulb glimmered and then glowed bright.

'It's working!' shouted Lotti, and then her face fell as the bulb began to spark before shattering entirely and exploding into flames on the bench.

At least one advantage of having a workbench made of ice was that the fire was short-lived – although it did melt a large dent into its surface.

'See?' sulked Zeina miserably.

'Hmm . . .' Lotti scratched behind one of her ears with her paw. 'It certainly works – just a little *too* well. Nothing we can't fix with a little tinkering.' She smiled, giving Zeina a gentle nudge.

They toiled together all afternoon, talking as they worked. Zeina told Lotti all about what happened last year, about Steele and the whale hunt and her aerocycle, which Lotti made her promise to show her before they left. Lotti told Zeina all about Palik and Valco Sol and the horned sky whales.

'Their tusks are one of the strongest materials on earth,' Lotti explained. 'It makes the most powerful weapons and the most precise tools.' She held up a tiny white screwdriver that she was using to adjust the quartz lens on Zeina's prototype.

'Doesn't it bother you?' Zeina asked, unable to hold back any longer. '*Hunting* the whales?'

'It did when I first came here,' Lotti replied. 'But the hunt isn't quite like the one you saw last year, remember. Especially now I designed this.'

She showed Zeina a metal box with knobs and dials a bit like a radio. On the top was a big gold funnel, like those Zeina had seen on Aboves' fancy music machines.

'It's called an echophone machine,' she said, her eyes gleaming with excitement. 'It works using the same wavelength as the whale's natural communication system. It makes a vibration in the air that the sky whales can hear as a message. It kind of . . . calls to them, I suppose.'

Lotti flicked a switch and turned one of the knobs. Zeina could see the gold funnel begin to vibrate slightly, and yet she could not hear a thing.

'I can't hear anything at all,' Zeina frowned.

'Ah, human ears can't hear the vibrations from this machine or the messages sky whales sing to each other. Other species, Feln and Kotarth included, can hear and understand the whale song – that's how your friend Katu can track sky whales so easily. The Feln have used echolocation to help them hunt sky whales for years, but with this machine we can now target specific whales. It calls directly to the older whales near the end of their natural lives. We can trap just one whale and the others aren't affected at all.'

'Don't you find it sad?' Zeina asked, memories of Steele's whale hunt flashing into her mind.

Lotti frowned. 'Horned sky whales have been an important part of the Feln livelihood since the beginning of time. Their meat and blubber, plus the preserves, pickles and juices we make out of the lilaberries, are the only way we survive the winter.'

Following a moment of silence, Lotti suggested they take a little break and poured herself and Zeina a cup of lilaberry juice each. 'To new friends, and new discoveries!' She held up her cup to Zeina's.

Zeina smiled and bumped Lotti's cup in a toast. Immediately, she knew she had miscalculated Lotti's strength and the cup slipped out of her hand.

'Oh no!' Zeina cried, as dark-purple juice sloshed out of her cup and on to the black material covering the quartz of her prototype, soaking it entirely. She threw off the material, rushing to wipe up the juice from the surface of the quartz with the sleeve of her coat.

'Zeina, stop, look!' Lotti grabbed her arm. At first, Zeina couldn't comprehend what she was seeing. The little lightbulb was burning brightly and evenly for the first time . . . *ever*.

'What?' Zeina stared in amazement. 'That doesn't make *any* sense.'

'No . . .' Lotti's whiskers twitched, her pupils narrowed into thin daggers in a way that reminded Zeina of Katu. 'It does!' She held her paw high over the surface of the quartz and used her other to wipe away the dark juice. The paw over the prototype flinched and withdrew as the clean quartz flashed in the sunlight and the bulb responded as before – by exploding.

'See!' she said, grey eyes dancing with triumph.

Zeina frowned. She didn't see anything at all! Lotti hurriedly went over to her shelves, rifling through a box until she found what she was looking for. She brought over a little glass vial filled with purple dye.

'This is a dye made from lilaberries,' she explained. 'It reacts with heat and light rays in a very particular way. In the past I've used it to develop lots of things, from invisible ink to sunscreen.'

Lotti unscrewed the quartz lens and pipetted a few drops of the dye on to the surface of the titanium. Then with Zeina's help she screwed the lens back in place and set up the wires with a new bulb. Again, the bulb burned evenly.

'The dye stops the prototype from absorbing too much heat. The light rays it lets through can then be converted to electricity.' Lotti's ears flicked with excitement.

Gleefully, Zeina tested it by covering the quartz with her hand and then uncovering it, watching the bulb switch on and off as if attached to a switch. She couldn't believe they had finally found a way to get her solar tech to work!

By the time Zeina left the workshop the sun was beginning to set. She waved goodbye to Lotti, who had locked the prototype away until tomorrow when the new sun meant they would make their final tweaks.

The sweet smell of baked bread drifted round the corner, along with the laughter of Shrapnel. Her stomach growled. The dining room had been set up for afternoon tea with giant cake stands overflowing with pastries, waffles, tarts and sandwiches.

Zeina saw that she was the last to arrive, taking up the same dining chair with the miniature ice palace on its back next to Jackson. Nedra waved at her from across the table.

'Did you make any progress?' Zeina asked Jackson in a hushed whisper, raising her eyebrows in the direction of Nedra, who was now tucking into a particularly delicious-looking berry tart.

Jackson shook his head, looking crestfallen. 'She disappeared and I didn't get a chance to go after her. She came back about twenty minutes later and said she'd had to go back for her scarf.'

He flushed but Zeina was in far too good a mood to chastise him.

'Don't worry,' she winked. 'Now that my solar tech is working, we can devote all our spare time to investigating.'

'You finished it?' Jackson's eyes widened.

Zeina nodded, feeling elated. Things were finally going right for the first time in a long time, and her world seemed to buzz with possibilities. Her dad would be so pleased when he saw the solar tech working. Captain Parr would be able to impress the Emerald King and – with proof that humans and Feln *could* work well together – might even get her alliance. Now Zeina and Jackson could concentrate all their energy on finding proof that Nedra was Pseudonym.

The atmosphere around the table during tea was quite different to their awkward lunch. Filled with excitement from their afternoon activities, Smog Rats and Feln chatted, exchanging stories and sipping steaming cups of herbal tea from little decorated cups. Even Katu and the Emerald King managed a few polite words to each other, and Captain Parr laughed with Zeina's dad as he recounted how Shrapnel had crashed into a pile of snow, trying to beat him in a Glindaski race. There was even a roar of hearty laughter from Commander Hugrak, followed by an all-powerful blow as he banged his paw on the table in merriment.

And then from somewhere above, another noise.

The crack of breaking ice.

'Zeina!' came the unmistakeable voice of Sparks, her enormous eyes focused on the ceiling. A large crack had formed in the ice holding up the chandelier directly above Zeina's head. She felt frozen to her chair somehow, unable to move, unable to do anything but stare up at the huge crystal structure as it tinkled and then shook and then began to fall.

Her father hurried to his feet but it was obvious he wouldn't make it to her in time. It was then that Katu leapt into action, pouncing across the table, knocking Zeina backwards from her chair and out of the way, just in time. Half a second longer and Zeina would have been crushed by the chandelier, which landed with an almighty crash, sending shards of ice across the room.

There was the sound of chairs scraping on the floor, shrieks of astonishment, cries of pain and then an icy silence.

CHAPTER 10

The image of the falling chandelier haunted Jackson's dreams for much of the night. He saw it fall, again and again, each time in slow motion while he sat unable to do anything but stare up at it, paralysed in fear. Crash. Crash. Crash. Over and over again, that fatal sound, slicing through the air above their heads and then smashing into a hundred pieces, each deadly sharp.

Thank goodness for Katu.

Katu had saved Zeina's life, and maybe Jackson's too. His pounce had knocked Zeina out of her chair, just moments before it was completely crushed by the falling chandelier. This action had snapped Jackson out of his terror. He sprang backwards and cowered, his arms shielding his face, as the ice splinters flew in all directions across the room.

Not everyone had been so lucky. Directly across the table from them, Sparks and Nedra had cuts to their hands and arms, Asher had a bruise on his head where a particularly large crystal had fallen from the chandelier as he'd tried to get to Zeina, and Shrapnel a savage slice across his cheekbone that had needed stitches. He had lost a lot of blood. Parr had said that just a centimetre higher and he might have lost his eye.

But no one was as badly injured as Katu, who in knocking Zeina clear had been ensnared himself by the great chandelier. In the chaos after the fall, Katu managed to wriggle one leg free but the other was trapped completely. The Emerald King, his crown knocked to the floor, roared for his guards to get Lotti, who came running with eyes as round as a winter moon, to free Katu with her tools.

It had taken half an hour of careful chipping away at the ice before Katu was freed. His head was in a tearful Zeina's lap as he tried his hardest to not flinch with every shard that Lotti removed. But it was immediately clear that his leg was badly injured.

Jackson had caught a glimpse of it, bent at an odd angle, before Lotti and Parr manoeuvred it back into shape and bound it up tightly with a splint. Katu and Shrapnel had been given something to help them sleep and put to bed in the hospital wing.

After what felt like only a few minutes of fretful sleep, Jackson gave up and pushed himself down his tunnel into the communal area. It seemed that he wasn't the only one who had found sleeping difficult as awake already, and gathered around the little stove, were Sparks, Zeina, Asher, Nedra and Parr. They talked in low voices, the light from the little window signalling that dawn would soon be upon them.

'Morning, Jackson,' said Parr, her brow furrowed. 'Come by the stove. There's warm milk.'

Jackson sat next to Zeina and Sparks, covering his legs with the same blanket that covered theirs. He sipped the milk, which was sweet and warm.

Zeina's arm soothed Sparks's shoulders. 'If you hadn't called out like that when you did, we would have been crushed.'

Sparks sniffed, tears falling down pale, terrified cheeks as she scribbled on to her writing pad.

I COULDN'T GET THE WORDS OUT. I SHOULD HAVE WARNED YOU SOONER.

Jackson shook his head. 'You saved us, Sparks.'

He looked at the others.

'Come on, Nedra,' Asher said, filling up her cup with more steaming milk. 'You just need some sleep.'

Nedra's hat was pulled down low over a red and blotchy face. Why was she so upset? For a moment Jackson thought she might have turned herself in, admitted to Parr that she was Pseudonym, but as Asher patted her back the reason she was crying soon became clear.

Nedra sniffed and looked up at him. 'He could have lost his eye.'

Asher nodded. 'But he didn't. Shrapnel is a tough one. He's had injuries worse than this before. Believe me, he'll be back to his normal, snarky self by the Equinox, I promise.'

As soon as the sun had risen, they all went to the hospital wing. It was the only part of the Glacial Palace constructed of anything other than ice or snow. The walls and roof were made of wood, covered in a thick layer of earth and moss on the outside and layers of furs on the inside, meaning it was much warmer than any other part of the palace. Down the centre of the room were a number of raised wooden bunks arranged in rows, but only two were occupied.

Waving at them from the first bunk was Shrapnel. His eye was almost swollen shut from a large cut underneath, which oozed slightly, but he seemed back to full spirits, just as Zeina's dad had promised. Zeina gave him an enormous hug while Nedra and Sparks busied themselves around him, handing him hot drinks and food, and making sure he had enough blankets.

'I could get used to this,' he smiled.

Katu looked very small curled up on his bunk, his bandaged leg stretched out in front of him, but he was alive. Zeina cried as she thanked him, stroking his paw.

He smiled weakly. 'I'm just glad you're OK. Now, I must speak to our captain a while.'

Jackson watched Parr and Katu talk in whispers. Katu's ears flicked, his furry eyebrows knotted as he spoke. He tried to sit up, wincing in pain, groaning with the effort.

'No more now, Katu. You must rest,' said Parr. Jackson only caught fragments: 'Tomorrow . . . can discuss . . . still time.'

They waved goodbye to the patients and made their way back to their quarters, where awaiting them was a gift hamper that would rival anything Jackson had seen in Ravenport: baskets crammed with fruits; platters of pastries and puddings; flagons of lilaberry wine; beautiful arrangements of flowers; and, right at the front, a golden card with an embossed emblem of the Glacial Palace.

'Maybe chandeliers should fall from the sky more often!' Nedra joked, some of her usual spirit restored since seeing Shrapnel alive and well.

Parr studied the card carefully as the rest tucked into the tempting treats.

'The king sends his good wishes and has invited us all to his throne room tomorrow at sunrise. You will need to bring your solar tech, Zeina. Is it ready?'

'Almost,' Zeina replied, wiping crumbs from her mouth. 'I'll finish it in Lotti's workshop this afternoon.'

'Good,' Parr nodded. 'Your father will go with you. He can help with those finishing touches. I know he's been dying to see your progress.'

Zeina smiled through a mouthful of cake.

'What else does it say, Parr?' Jackson asked, gesturing to the card.

In reply, Parr handed him the note.

Captain Parr,

I hope you will accept this hamper as a token of my deepest condolences. In the hundreds of years the Feln have constructed a winter Glacial Palace, we have never had an accident such as this one. I am most troubled that such an incident has occurred while you are visiting.

May I reassure you that instructions have been given this morning for all the palace's decorations to be checked – every chandelier, every pillar, every ice window – and for everything to be reinforced with fresh ice from the Kalder River if necessary. Thankfully, my servants tell me that the boy and Prince Katu will make a full recovery. The braveness he showed in sacrificing his own safety for others must be honoured.

May I invite you and your crew to attend my throne room at sunrise tomorrow. Bring your innovators and their new technology so that I may have a demonstration.

Emerald King

It amused Jackson that the king should refer to Shrapnel as 'the boy'. He made a mental note to tell Shrapnel next time he saw him.

'What does this mean?' Jackson asked Parr. 'Does the king propose to make an alliance with us after all?'

Parr had taken off her mechanical arm. She retrieved a little pot of grease from her jacket and began to rub it into the metal joints and springs, bending each finger joint in turn. Jackson knew that this was what Parr liked to do when she was thinking.

'Perhaps he has begun to appreciate Katu's warnings about how the climate is changing up here,' she replied. 'Or maybe he just wants the solar technology, now he's heard from Lotti that it actually works. We won't know until tomorrow.'

Parr focused on the steel tendons that fanned across the palm of her hand. She was quiet for a while, working in the grease as she thought, a deep frown appearing on her brow.

Fastening her arm back into place, she exhaled. 'It seems this accident has shaken the king. I hope this meeting is a good sign, but we are fast running out of time. The Equinox is the day after tomorrow and then we leave. If an alliance is to be agreed, it has to be tomorrow.' Her eye gaped at Jackson, intense and pleading. 'I know I haven't been very open with you, lad, and I'm sorry. The world is a dangerous place for us Smog Rats – but it will be much safer once we have the support of the Feln. You will help me, Jackson, won't you?'

Jackson felt a sudden rush of affection for this woman who had taken him in when he had nothing and no one. He might not agree with all of her decisions but he trusted her.

He nodded. 'Of course, Captain.'

CHAPTER 11

'Zeina!' Her dad's voice stirred her from sleep. 'Wake up! You need to get dressed and fetch your prototype from the workshop. We're due in the throne room in half an hour.'

Zeina looked at her wrist where her pocket watch told her it was only five a.m.

'But it's *so* early,' she yawned.

'The Equinox is tomorrow, remember. Sunrise gets earlier every day – by this time tomorrow the sun will already be up!'

Quickly she dressed and ran along to the workshop. Lotti smiled as she handed the prototype case over.

'Don't be nervous. We got it working perfectly yesterday. I *know* the king is going to be impressed,' she purred. 'See you in there!'

Zeina's heart fluttered as they entered the throne room. It was a shame that Shrapnel and Katu were still recovering in

114

the hospital wing, but everyone else was there and even Captain Parr seemed to hum with excitement.

The king sat tall on his ice throne, stroking his bearded chin. The green jewels of his crown gleamed proudly. His eyes, beady black, narrowed as they approached his throne.

'Good morning, Emerald King,' said Parr with a little bow.

The king growled. Something was wrong. Lotti stood beside the throne, but Zeina noticed her demeanour had changed completely.

'It is a most *unfortunate* morning,' the king snarled, 'for all of us.'

'Oh,' Parr faltered. 'The incident with the chandelier must have been as terrifying for you and the Feln who live here at the palace as it was for us, Emerald King, but I thought perhaps – after your kind gift and note – that it had at least highlighted why we must work together.' Parr's voice was strong and powerful, but Zeina could tell by the way she flexed and straightened the fingers of her mechanical hand that she was nervous.

'HA!' the king snarled. 'A broken chandelier is the least of *both* our worries, Captain. I admit that yesterday my views on an alliance were beginning to change. Lotti was singing the praises of Miss Starborn and her solar tech, and I was impressed by how your crew took care of each other when

115

they were put in danger. But I can see now that we were *both* taken in. If you think I would ever form an alliance with someone who would write these dreadful lies about me and my kingdom, you are sorely mistaken.'

Parr stepped back, aghast.

'I'm afraid I have no idea what you're talking about.'

The king gestured to a servant, who came forward with a newspaper for Parr.

THE SMOG SCOOP
Know the truth, trust the revolution

AIRSHIPS OVER PALIK

After a worryingly mild winter across the Northern Continent, the Feln of Palik had cause to be further concerned this week, when human airships were spotted in the region. Airships have been banned from travelling north of Palik City following an agreement made with infamous explorer Vivianne Steele more than ten years ago. Following her death and the recent ascent of a new Feln king, residents of Palik have been worried that the agreement may not stand and it would seem, after sightings of an Upper Atmosphere airship just this week, that their concerns may have merit.

'We don't want humans here,' stated one resident, who preferred to remain anonymous. 'Already our ice plains are thinning. I worry our continent will end up just like our friends' in the west, the Kotarth, if our king doesn't show his strength.' Another reported that their children were terrified when they spotted the airship. 'They asked me what it meant and I didn't know what to tell them!' they recounted.

It has been made clear to this publication that many Feln share these worries. The pollution that has destroyed the Eastern, Western and Southern Continents could soon begin to impact the north, with devastating effects for our world. If Above families seek to find new mining grounds to replace the ones reclaimed in the west, then the north is in imminent danger. We must all come together to stop this immediately.

Pseudonym

'This is *nothing* to do with us,' Parr said sternly, shaking the newspaper at the king, who huffed back, his teeth bared.

'It is named after you, is it not? You agree with what it says, do you not?' He arose from his throne. 'I believe *you* wrote this yourself, Captain Parr. You thought it would scare me into an alliance. Well, it has done the opposite.'

'That isn't true, Emerald King. I want to find Pseudonym just as much as—' Parr began.

'Making up these hateful lies from my subjects,' the king interrupted, pacing up and down and muttering to himself. 'No Feln would ever say such things about me. They love and trust their king.'

'But . . . there *was* an airship. Commander Hugrak saw it too,' Nedra piped up, and Zeina was relieved, for it was what she would have said if she'd been brave enough. Parr quickly pushed Nedra behind her as the king bounded over to them, roaring with such ferocity that his own guards flinched.

'AND I EXPLAINED THE AIRSHIP SIGHTING WAS NOTHING TO CONCERN YOURSELVES WITH. You humans always think you know best, don't you? Always think you can get your own way!'

Parr stood her ground against the giant king, her eye raised to meet his gaze. She spoke in a calm, low whisper. 'Whether or not these quotes are real, King, your subjects will be nervous – they know and love their home just as much as you do and they can see their land changing. BUT,' she lifted her hand to stop another ferocious onslaught, 'that is all beside the point because, like I said, *we* have nothing to do with this paper.' She gestured to include them all. '*We* didn't write this and *we* don't know who Pseudonym is!'

Jackson's cheeks flushed at this and he glanced nervously over at Zeina. She shook her head ever so slightly – now was not the time to tell Parr about their Nedra suspicions.

'It's true, Emerald King,' said Zeina's dad. 'Despite its name, this newspaper has nothing to do with Captain Parr or her Smog Rats.'

'What a strange coincidence then,' the king snarled smugly. 'This paper that you have *nothing to do with* writes about Palik, just when *you* have an airship there.'

Parr flushed, lowering her face to stare down at the paper again. 'I agree,' she said quietly. 'It's something I can no longer ignore.'

'If you wish to form an alliance, I demand that Pseudonym is found and brought to me immediately,' the king snarled. 'You will tell Commander Hugrak where you have hidden the *Nightjar* and he will take a team of my royal guards to question them.'

'No, that is *my* crew. I will go and investigate Pseudonym myself. Commander Hugrak can accompany me, if you insist.'

'Very well, but you only have until tomorrow evening. After the Equinox celebrations are finished you must leave my kingdom, and if there is no alliance by then, you will never return. Once Pseudonym is caught, they will be forced to print a retraction and will be put on trial here in Palik for treason.'

Parr nodded.

'It is only in the interests of my subjects that I don't banish you all this second. I admit, I was beginning to see the benefits of an alliance – protection against our common foes, sharing information and innovations.' His eyes glided over Zeina's prototype case. 'But I cannot join with those that I cannot trust.'

With that he gestured for the guards to escort them away. The two enormous ice doors slammed behind them.

Parr strode on ahead, Zeina's dad running to keep up with her. Some way behind them walked Nedra and Sparks, seemingly shocked into silence. Zeina and Jackson hung right at the very back.

'What shall we do?' Jackson whispered to Zeina. 'We have to tell Parr about our suspicions, don't we?'

'We can't, Jackson,' Zeina whispered back. 'We haven't got any proof that it even is Nedra. You heard Parr; she wants Pseudonym brought to justice and the king's so angry he will just blame whoever is brought to him.' She imagined Nedra on trial, surrounded by angry Feln. Nedra, who had spent years longing for freedom, locked up in a Feln prison. And all for just telling the truth!

'If it is Nedra, Parr isn't going to find Pseudonym back on the *Nightjar*. She has to give the king someone, or there'll be no alliance!' Jackson hissed.

Zeina felt torn; she knew how important the alliance was to the Smog Rats, yet she couldn't imagine giving Nedra up.

'We can talk to her while Parr is away. Confirm that she *is* Pseudonym,' Zeina said. 'Persuade her to come clean. Perhaps the king will take pity on her if she agrees to print a retraction. Parr is much more likely to defend her if she gives herself up.'

'And if she doesn't?'

'We've got twenty-four hours before the Equinox begins, if she doesn't hand herself in,' Zeina took in one deep breath, 'then we'll have no choice but to tell Parr our suspicions. But not before then, agreed?'

Jackson hesitated, his brows furrowed.

'Come on, Jackson. She's already been through so much. Just like you, she never really had a family until she became part of the Smog Rats. We can't take that away from her without giving her a chance.'

'OK,' he huffed. 'But just until the sun rises tomorrow morning. If she hasn't given herself up by then, we'll do it for her. Agreed?'

'Agreed.'

Back in their quarters, Parr was seething. She held up the article for them all to see, staring at each of them in turn, her eye dark and dangerous.

'What did I say about the *Smog Scoop*? Truth or not, this article has cost us the alliance, which puts all our lives in danger! I didn't want to entertain the notion that Pseudonym was part of my crew, but after this . . .' She looked down at the headline in disgust. 'I can't believe anyone would ignore my orders so plainly. Someone must know something.'

Everyone shook their heads. Zeina, her eyes completely focused on Nedra, couldn't detect any shadow of guilt or regret. She appeared just as shocked as the rest of them.

'If any of you know anything about this, you must tell me *now*,' Parr repeated.

'You won't be in trouble,' Zeina's dad added gently. 'But we need to know.'

They all shook their heads again. Zeina hoped Parr couldn't hear her heart hammering against her breastbone. She hated lying to her dad. But she also felt Nedra deserved another chance.

'What's your plan, Parr?' asked Jackson, once it was obvious no one was going to come forward.

'I have no choice,' said Parr, shaking her head. 'I must return to the *Nightjar* with Hugrak and question the crew.'

'The king was furious,' Zeina whispered. 'Even if Pseudonym apologises and promises to print a retraction, won't they be punished?'

'Well, maybe they should have thought about that *before* they went against my direct orders!' Parr shouted, shaking the paper in frustration. 'It's not just the king who is furious. This article tells the world about where *we* are right now. It's put us *all* in danger. Another reason why I need to return to the *Nightjar* is to check that the crew are safe. I will do my best to protect Pseudonym from the king, but that's it – they'll be out of the Smog Rats for good.'

Sparks scribbled on her notepad and held it up for Parr to see.

WHAT IF YOU CAN'T FIND THEM?

'Someone in Palik has given away *this* information,' she flicked the paper viciously. 'Be that Pseudonym or one of their secret reporters, *that* person needs to apologise and put things right.'

'I think it's best if I accompany you, Parr,' Zeina's dad piped up, much to Zeina's horror.

'What? Dad, no,' Zeina said, before she could stop herself. She couldn't stand the thought of her dad taking the dangerous journey there and back in a day.

He crouched down so his eyes were level with hers. 'Parr will need help, Zeina. It's going to be tight getting to Palik, questioning the crew and getting back before the celebrations start tomorrow morning.'

'Thank you, Asher,' said Parr. 'But what about the children? Katu isn't well enough to be left in charge and Shrapnel is still resting.'

'Nedra, how do you feel about being in charge while we're gone?' He smiled encouragingly at Nedra, and she flushed.

'I—Of course, Mr Starborn,' she said.

Parr hastily examined her pocket watch. 'That's settled then. Nedra, go and see Shrapnel and Katu and let them know what has happened, OK? Under no circumstances are they to leave the hospital wing, understood?'

Nedra, her fingers twisting around the cuffs of her woollen coat, nodded solemnly. 'Of course, Captain. I'll go at once.'

'I'll ask Lotti to come and check on you all later,' Parr added. 'And we'll leave Albi behind. If there's any trouble at all, remember you can send him and he can get a message to us in Palik within the hour.'

124

Zeina's dad scratched his long beard. 'I want you lot to promise to stay within our quarters, Lotti's workshop and the hospital wing, OK? No wandering around.'

The children all nodded begrudgingly.

Zeina felt more torn than ever as she, Jackson and Sparks helped her dad load up the Glindaski with everything he, Parr and Hugrak would need. Despite having the commander as their guide across the ice plain, the journey was still full of potential dangers – a hidden crevasse, an avalanche, a snowstorm.

'Cheer up!' Her dad cupped her cold cheeks in his gloved hands. 'I'll be back before you know it.'

Zeina's breath turned to steam against the freezing air. 'You'll be careful, won't you?'

'I'm always careful. And just think, if we're successful, twenty-four hours from now we can celebrate *both* the Equinox and a new alliance. Your solar prototype will be ready—' His eyebrows knitted together as he glanced around. 'Speaking of which, where *is* your prototype case, Zeina? In all the excitement, I quite forgot about it.'

'I put it back in Lotti's workshop.'

He scratched his salt-and-pepper beard, peering at her over his spectacles. 'Might be worth asking Lotti if you can move it to our quarters. Hide it somewhere in one of the sleeping pods. Make sure that it's locked and keep the key on you at all times, OK? We don't know who else has a key to Lotti's workshop and that invention of yours is going to revolutionise everything, I can feel it.'

Zeina smiled. It felt good to not have to lie to her dad about her solar tech at last. 'I will, Dad. I promise.'

'Make sure both patients stay in bed.' Parr made the children give their word. 'And you lot are to *stay safe*, that's an order!' she added, looking at each of them fiercely as they waved them off across the plain.

On the way back to their quarters, Zeina decided to visit Lotti's workshop, just as she had promised her dad.

'Come on, Jackson,' she said. 'I can give you a quick demonstration.'

'It definitely won't explode this time?' he asked hesitantly.

'No! It works really well now, honestly. Sparks, do you want to come?'

But Sparks shook her head, getting out her paper and writing 'GOING BACK TO SEE SHRAPNEL'. Zeina nodded and they waved her off. She was pale and worried, her eyes even larger than usual, but Zeina knew how much she cared about Shrapnel.

When they arrived at the workshop, it was open.

'Lotti?' Zeina called, but there was no answer.

126

'Maybe she's gone to check in on Katu,' Jackson suggested.

'Strange she didn't lock up her workshop though,' Zeina mused. Maybe her dad was right that her prototype would be safer in their quarters.

Lotti had looked so miserable standing next to the king as he berated them in his throne room. Maybe she was still there. She hoped the king hadn't somehow blamed Lotti for everything; it was Lotti who had persuaded him to allow the Smog Rats to visit Palik in the first place. 'Oh, look! Here's my case, just where I left it.'

She got out her little key to unlock the clasp, but the case simply swung open. She gasped, clutching on to Jackson's arm, all the colour drained from her face. The case was completely empty. Her prototype was gone!

CHAPTER 12

They searched Lotti's workshop from top to bottom. Jackson inspected her workbench, in between gadgets and discarded tools and behind every pile of papers. Zeina opened cupboards, scoured every shelf and even rummaged through drawers. Jackson had to stop her from actually tipping out the contents of each drawer on to the floor.

'But it's gone, Jackson! It's not here!' Zeina's eyes darted desperately around the room, her hands grasping her hair into disorderly tufts.

'I know, Zeina, but Lotti's not going to be very happy if we destroy her entire workshop!'

'Do you think *Lotti* could have taken it?' Zeina gasped.

'Not stolen it, no. But I suppose she might have hidden it for safekeeping?' Jackson replied. For some reason, Parr seemed to trust Lotti implicitly and Parr's trust was not easily earned. 'The workshop door was open, so I guess anyone could have taken it. Didn't you lock up the case?'

'I did.' Zeina frowned. 'Well, I'm almost certain I did.'

'Come on, wrecking this place isn't going to help. We need to find Lotti. If she's not here, maybe she went to see Katu in the hospital wing, like she promised Parr.'

They decided to go to the hospital wing via the throne room. Zeina was worried the king might be holding Lotti there as some kind of punishment for ever recommending that he invited the Smog Rats to Palik.

Two Feln warriors stood guard outside the tall ice doors of the throne room. One held a white spear, the other a drum that she struck with a steady rhythm. The corridors around them echoed with the same beat.

'What's going on?' Zeina asked, marching up to the warrior with the spear, who moved it across the doors to bar the way.

'The king has put the palace on lockdown,' he barked without looking down at them. 'Everyone is to return to their quarters and stay there.'

'Why?' Zeina exclaimed, trying to get closer to the doors, where they could make out only shadows moving behind the thick ice.

'That is not for you to know, *human*,' he snapped. 'Return to your quarters at once, otherwise I'm sure we can find somewhere else to put you.'

'Come on, Zeina.' Jackson pulled her away before she got herself arrested. He hadn't liked the way the guard's eyes glinted as he said the word 'human'. 'We were looking for Lotti. Can you at least tell us if she's in there?' Jackson asked him as politely as he could.

The warrior with the drum seemingly took pity on them. 'The king's innovator is advising him on a security issue,' she said, eyeing her companion carefully. 'You young ones must return to your quarters *now*, and stay there until you hear the drums cease.'

Despite the guards' advice, they decided to go to the hospital wing as planned – they had to tell Shrapnel and Katu about what they had seen. Jackson's heart raced as he tried to keep up with Zeina, who would only slow intermittently to peek around corners and check for guards up ahead. She needn't have bothered; apart from the drumming that got louder and then faded as they journeyed across the palace, everywhere was strangely silent and deserted.

Their panic mounted as they reached the hospital wing, for it too was abandoned. Shrapnel wasn't in his bunk; there was no sign of Nedra, Sparks or Lotti; and even more worryingly, Katu was missing too.

'Maybe they moved everyone back to our quarters when the king issued a lockdown?' suggested Zeina, although she sounded as unconvinced as Jackson felt. A shiver went through him despite the warmth of the cosy hospital wing.

The full weight of their situation struck them when they arrived in their quarters. There was no sign of their friends; no one sleeping in any of the dens and no one gathered around the stove, the embers of which were beginning to burn out. It suggested to Jackson that it had been left unattended for hours. He drew his coat tightly around himself and threw another log on to the fire. It was getting cold and soon it would be dark. Through the window he could see the sun was so low that it touched the ice plain, forming pink and orange flames across the sky.

'Jackson, what is going on?' Zeina exclaimed, shaking her head. 'Where is everyone?'

'I don't know,' Jackson replied. They hadn't eaten since breakfast and his stomach growled noisily. Something else wasn't right – it took him a moment or two to work out exactly what it was. The distant rhythm of the drums still beat in the background, but their quarters themselves were eerily quiet. A curious thought tugged at him.

'Zeina – the aviary! Come on!' He grabbed Zeina by the hand and they ran.

Jackson's fears were confirmed when they reached the aviary – something indeed was very, VERY wrong. Usually it was bustling with noisy birds, cawing and flapping over scraps of fish. But today it was completely silent and, save for a few scattered feathers on the floor, it too was empty. Every single perch was deserted.

They stood, their hands clutched together, eyes wide in horror.

Zeina went over to inspect the chute that led to the outside – but a great boulder of snow and ice had been placed over the exit and no amount of pushing would shift it.

'What do we do, Jackson?' Zeina gulped. 'Someone has got rid of all the ice ravens, my prototype has been stolen, everyone is missing and we can't even send Albi for help!' She bit her lip, tears brimming in her eyes.

Jackson hated it when Zeina cried; it didn't happen very often and so when it did it made him panic. He began to shiver, his head spinning. Should they go back to the throne room? Demand to speak to the Emerald King? Had poor Katu and the others been captured and locked up the minute Captain Parr and Asher had left? Were he and Zeina next?

Hurried footsteps along the corridor made them both duck behind the ravens' pedestal. Peeking through, Jackson could make out a dark shadow, silhouetted against the light from the corridor. The thick ice of the pedestal distorted them, making it impossible to tell if it was Feln or human, but they were completely silent, searching for something or someone, and they were getting closer and closer.

Jackson held his breath. His mouth was dry and his own heartbeat thundered in his ears. Zeina caught his eye. She had stopped crying, her expression now fixed and determined. She put a finger to her mouth, counted out 'One, two, three' using her fingers and then mouthed one word: 'RUN'.

Jackson nodded to show he understood. It didn't sound like much of a plan to him, but it was their only choice.

The shadow was now right in front of the pedestal, blocking out any light from the corridor outside the aviary.

Silently, Zeina mouthed, 'One ... Two ... Three' and then dashed out from behind the pedestal, running as quickly as she could for the exit. Jackson tried to do the same but his way was blocked.

'Ah!' cried out the shadow, who tripped over Jackson's foot and fell to the floor with a thud. 'Ow!'

'Shrapnel?'

'As if I didn't have enough injuries already!' Shrapnel replied, rubbing his head.

'Oh, thank goodness you're safe!' Zeina cried.

'No thanks to you two!' he grumbled. 'Where have you been? We've been searching the palace for you. I woke up to find that Katu had gone. The palace is deserted, there's that strange drumming and someone has got rid of all the ravens too!'

133

'Who is *we*?' asked Jackson. 'Nedra was supposed to come and see you hours ago.'

Shrapnel wrinkled his nose and then winced, his hand going up to the bulging stitches across his cheek. 'I haven't seen Ned at all today. Sparks was there when I woke up, Katu was already gone, and we've been looking for you two ever since! She's sneaked back down to Lotti's workshop now to see if you've turned up. I said I'd have one last check here. What's happened to the ravens?'

'Someone's scared them off and then blocked the chute from the outside with snow,' Zeina explained.

There was a scuffle as Sparks appeared in the doorway. Breathless from running, she panted, holding up one of the whale-blubber-powered lamps from the hospital wing.

'Sparks? Are you OK?' asked Jackson. She was shifting from foot to foot, like she did when she had something really important to say. Desperately she searched for her notepad, patting down her pockets with her free hand but to no avail. Jackson came in close so that she could whisper to him. Her lips pursed, her eyes wide, she took a deep breath and spoke. Jackson could feel the huge effort it took to get every word out.

'Katu's . . . been . . . kidnapped.'

'What? By who? Where did you see him?' Zeina demanded, for she had craned her head as close as she dared, in order to overhear.

'Zeina!' Jackson and Shrapnel shouted in unison.

'Just give her a chance,' Jackson added gently.

Sparks nodded and took another deep breath, talking quietly but to all three of them this time.

'Workshop window . . . Lotti and a guard . . . took Katu to a Glindaski . . . Lotti had a pistol.'

CHAPTER 13

I n a matter of moments they had donned their extra
layers, snow boots and hats, grabbed their packs and
made their way outside. The exit where the Glindaskis
were kept under shelter had been left curiously unguarded.
There was no trace of Emerald Fire in the sky tonight. Great
grey clouds swirled over the moon and blocked out the
stars. The first few flakes of fresh snow began to powder the
ground.

Sparks pointed to where she had seen Lotti and the guard
take Katu, and there, cut into the snow, were tracks leading
away from the shelter. Zeina noticed that, unlike the tracks
from the Glindaski that had, hours ago, taken Parr and her
dad south to Palik, these ones were freshly made with distinct
edges, and they led north.

'So what do we do?' Jackson asked, holding up the lamp
and squinting into the distance.

'We have to follow!' Zeina cried. 'There's no time to lose.'

The tracks were easy to see for the moment, but they would quickly fade as soon as the snow got any heavier.

'Even if we do manage to catch them, what's our plan?' Jackson said, his voice shaky against the ominous wind. 'Sparks said Lotti had a *pistol*.'

Sparks nodded when he looked to her for confirmation.

'What are we going to do against two Feln and a pistol?' Jackson continued.

'We'll think of something.' Zeina waved her arms in irritation. Jackson was often far too sensible – sometimes you just had to *do* first and *think* later.

'We can't follow them,' came Shrapnel's voice from the shelter.

Zeina turned on him. 'Shrapnel! It's *Katu*. Think of all the times he's put his neck on the line for us!'

'No, I mean we actually *can't* follow them,' he said, inspecting the back of the two remaining Glindaskis in the shelter. 'Come and see.'

They all crowded round the machines. The cages that contained the propellers had been forced open and the propellers inside smashed. Zeina examined one closely – two of its blades hung cracked and broken, and the third was bent out of shape. There was no way the damage had been caused accidentally – they had been sabotaged on purpose.

'Do you think Lotti did this?' Jackson asked, his brows furrowed.

'It doesn't matter,' Shrapnel replied, scratching his head. 'These aren't going to get us anywhere. And there's no way we'll ever make it on foot.'

'Could you fix it, Zeina?' Jackson asked hopefully.

Zeina examined the blades. Gently she turned the central rotor, causing one of them to fall off completely with a thud into the snow. 'Nope – not without a new propeller, and I didn't see any of this size in Lotti's workshop.'

'Hey, you two have your aerocycles with you, don't you?' Shrapnel asked, pointing at Zeina and Jackson.

'Yes, but they won't fly here, remember?' Zeina sighed. 'Once they're in the air, they run on cycle power, but the smog chamber gives them the boost they need to get airborne and there isn't enough smog in the atmosphere this far north.'

They fell silent, all hopelessly staring at the broken Glindaskis.

'Blubber?' Sparks's voice was a whisper against the wind. 'Blubber!' she repeated, louder and firmer, her eyes wide, pointing at the chamber where Commander Hugrak had set alight the little square of dried blubber to get the Glindaskis to start.

Zeina examined the chamber – it was roughly the same

size as the smog chamber and the fittings were remarkably similar. It was worth a shot!

'Yes,' she nodded, trying to convince herself more than the others around her. 'I think I can do it.' Her heartbeat thundered in her ears – she had to do it, for Katu. 'Jackson, go and get our aerocycles. Sparks, come with me to get the tools we'll need from the workshop.'

'I'll get some of those dried blubber cubes,' Shrapnel said. 'There were some lamps in the hospital wing. And I'll leave a note for Ned in her den, in case she comes back and wonders where we've all gone.'

They set about retrieving everything they needed and met back in the shelter. Shrapnel helped Zeina prise the blubber chamber off one of the Glindaskis and then held a lamp over her aerocycle while she worked. Sparks handed her tools, nuts and bolts as she asked for them. Clanks and bangs echoed across the white landscape.

It was then that Jackson noticed that the blubber chamber from the second Glindaski was missing. He found it lying in the snow, dented on one side and a big crack across where the blubber cube should be placed.

'What are we going to do?' he asked Zeina, bringing her the broken chamber. 'One aerocycle won't take all four of us.'

'We'll have to piggyback them,' Zeina replied, looking up briefly from the metal she was hammering into place. 'Use this aerocycle to get the other one into the air and then pedal really hard to keep it up.'

Jackson grimaced. Even after all the aerocycle flying he had done since joining the Smog Rats, Zeina knew that he was still terrified of falling.

'How much longer, Zee?' Shrapnel asked, watching the snow, which had now turned from a light powder into large feathery flakes.

Zeina screwed the last bolt tightly into place. 'Done!'

After some discussion, it was agreed that first Zeina and Shrapnel would set off on the adapted blubber-powered aerocycle and that Jackson and Sparks would ride on the one piggybacking behind. Jackson was the fastest at pedalling and it was thought that Shrapnel would weigh down the second aerocycle too much as a passenger. They set the aerocycles up, Zeina's ahead with two long ropes attaching it to the handlebars of Jackson's aerocycle behind.

Zeina took a deep breath and nodded at Shrapnel, who put the cube into the chamber and set it alight.

WHOOSH!

Up launched the aerocycle with such speed that Shrapnel had to grab on to Zeina's waist to stop him from falling off. She pedalled forward and up as hard as she could, but Jackson and Sparks simply dragged along the snow-covered ground behind them. There was a puff of black smoke from the chamber, that horrible sickly-sweet smell of burning fat and then the rope pulled Zeina's aerocycle backwards. She watched the moonlit clouds disappear from her reach as she and Shrapnel fell to the cold, hard ground.

Ooof.

'Is everyone OK?' Jackson asked.

'Peachy,' Shrapnel groaned, rubbing his thigh.

Snowflakes twirled in a race to meet the ground. The tracks nearest the shelter were beginning to disappear.

'We need someone to run along and then jump to get the pedals clear of the ground,' Jackson explained. 'I can't push off and pedal at the same time, but Sparks is too short.'

'Let's try swapping Shrapnel and Sparks then,' Zeina said quickly. She hated the thought of Katu injured and taken hostage. Who knows where they were planning on taking him. They had to get going, *now*.

It took only a few minutes to get everything set up again. This time Sparks held the blubber cube and got it ready to light. Shrapnel held on tightly to the second aerocycle and prepared to run. Jackson, feet on the pedals, was pale but had a look of steadfast determination on his face.

'Ready, steady, go!' he shouted.

But as the blubber cube burst into flames and Zeina began to pedal, there was another sound from below. The enormous doors of the Glacial Palace shook open with an icy crack and out came four Feln warriors. They caught a glimpse of the aerocycles and made for them at full speed, spears at the ready.

'Ah!' cried Shrapnel, his and Jackson's aerocycle desperately trying to keep up with Zeina's along the ground. 'Go, Zeina! Go!'

She turned away and fiercely pedalled upwards against the falling snow. The rope grew taut and for a moment she was sure they would crash again to the ground, get captured by the guards and never see Katu again.

Zeina roared her battle cry into the wind. The aerocycle carrying her and Sparks launched even higher into the sky. She felt the tension in the ropes slacken and turned her head again, terrified that they had lost Jackson and Shrapnel to the guards.

But, sure enough, there behind them was the second aerocycle, bobbing up and down just a few metres behind her own, the ropes still attached. Jackson smiled, red-faced and sweating, pedalling with all his might. Shrapnel leaned over to wave down at the Feln guards, who stood by the shelter looking up in confusion as the children escaped into sky.

CHAPTER 14

The snowstorm teased them, getting heavier and then – just when they thought they couldn't pedal any longer – easing off slightly. The moment they began to hope they had seen the worst of it, a torrent would come down again even thicker than before. Now released from their ropes, Jackson and Zeina took it in turns to fly close the ground and check that they were still following the tracks left by the Glindaski. Despite the lamp Shrapnel had hung from the aerocycle's handlebars, it was getting harder and harder to make out the tracks. Jackson worried that every time it was his turn to fly down, he would not have the strength to fly back up again against the wild wind that whipped at his face and froze his knuckles to the handlebars, even through his thick woollen gloves.

There was a sudden flurry so thick that Jackson could see nothing at all, and then the lamp from Zeina's aerocycle glimmered through the swirls of white like a beacon. He followed it down to the ground where Zeina and Sparks zigzagged desperately, searching for any sign of the tracks.

'It's no use,' Zeina shouted above the howl of the wind. 'They're gone!'

Too scared that if they stopped they would never be able to get Jackson's aerocycle back up in the air, they flew round and round in circles while they debated what to do next.

'Should we carry on north? Or head south to Palik?' Shrapnel bellowed. 'There's no way we can go back to the palace with those guards waiting for us.'

'We might have to. We'll never make it all the way to Palik,' Jackson puffed. His legs were burning, and he could see that Zeina was beginning to suffer too.

Sparks scowled into the storm, her eyes focusing on something Jackson couldn't yet make out. Suddenly she gasped, tapped Zeina frantically on the shoulder and pointed.

A flicker of silvery white flashed against the dark clouded sky. It disappeared and then appeared again, bigger and brighter. Soon it held still long enough for Jackson to make out two large white wings, a beak and two white feathered feet.

'It's Albi!' Zeina puffed, a big smile illuminating her face.

The bird fluttered in front of them, cawing and croaking. To Jackson his black eyes seemed to demand answers from them. *And where have* you *been?* they glinted angrily. Albi swooped up and then hovered. A harsh caw seemed to beckon them.

'I think . . . he wants us to follow him?' Jackson said slowly.

They flew to meet him and he swooped away, cawing until they caught up with him again. After a number of swoops and caws, Albi seemed satisfied that they could keep up and he set off into a continuous flight, Zeina just short of his tail feathers and Jackson flying closely behind. His wings sailed through the snowstorm with ease.

The ice plain below them began to undulate into steep peaks and deep icefalls. Albi weaved them around the gaping inky cracks that snaked across the white landscape and high above the spiked shadows of dark forests. It seemed as if they had been flying for hours. Jackson's hands felt stiff on the golden handlebars. He could feel Shrapnel shivering at his back.

Eventually Albi began to slow and then dived towards the edge of an enormous crack across the plain. The crevasse was much larger than the one they had seen on the day they arrived at the Glacial Palace – two towering cliff faces, metres apart, staring each other down. The chasm between them seemed endless. Albi hovered above the cliff and began a rough, impatient cawing. For a moment Jackson could not see why that particular part of the cliff was of any interest to

Albi. But then he spotted deep, deep down in the crevice a Glindaski-shaped speck.

'Look!' he cried. 'It's them!'

On a narrow ledge of ice, the Glindaski balanced precariously. Three little figures raised their faces to the sky – Katu, Lotti and a Feln guard. His green and gold cape billowed behind him in the wind.

Zeina started off in a dive towards them.

'Wait!' Jackson called. 'What about the pistol, Zeina? Don't get too close!'

As was so often the case, whether Zeina hadn't heard or was simply choosing to ignore him remained a mystery to Jackson.

'We'd better follow them,' sighed Shrapnel.

Jackson swooped down, following Zeina and Sparks into the deep fissure. The cliff faces on either side seemed to press in closer, as if the chasm was going to consume them.

The figures on the ledge began waving frantically.

'Katu,' Zeina called. 'Are you OK?'

'I'm fine, Zeina,' he shouted back. 'But we must find a way to get out of here immediately.'

Somewhere close by, the cliff face began to shake, sending showers of snow and chunks of ice down into the bottomless rift.

'Where's the pistol?' yelled Shrapnel.

'Never mind about that now,' Katu said calmly. 'The ledge isn't stable. Just get us all out first.'

Jackson looked over to Zeina, who nodded, throwing Jackson one of the ropes they had used to get him up in the air. 'I'll get Katu first, OK?'

'We'll get Lotti. Then whoever has the most strength left can go back for the guard,' said Shrapnel.

Shrapnel tied the rope to the back of Jackson's aerocycle and Sparks did the same to Zeina's. Jackson watched Zeina fly close over the ledge, the rope lowered so that Katu could grab on with both paws. His injured leg was still bandaged up, but other than that he appeared unscathed. The rope swung dangerously in the storm, threatening to crash Katu against the cliff. Jackson was filled with relief once Katu had been hauled safely up to the top.

Now it was time for him to get Lotti. Jackson flew closer to the ledge, getting ready to lower the rope to her outstretched paws. Shrapnel put one hand on his shoulder, calling down sternly, 'It's your turn, Lotti, but throw the pistol down into the gap first.'

She shook her head. 'Shrapnel, I don't know what you—'

'Throw the pistol, or else you're staying where you are,' Shrapnel called sharply.

With a growling huff, she did as he said and the gun disappeared into the ceaseless blue fissure. Once Lotti had grabbed on to the lowered rope, it took all of Jackson's strength to lift her up to the top of the cliff.

Zeina was already hovering back over the crevasse, sizing up the remaining guard.

'He's much bigger than either Katu or Lotti,' Zeina called breathlessly.

'We could – lift him together?' suggested Jackson, his lungs burning with the effort it took to speak. His legs were jelly. His feet kept slipping off the pedals.

The two aerocycles flew close together, Sparks and Shrapnel holding on around each other's waists to keep them steady. The guard roared as he grabbed on tightly, one rope for each of his front paws. He was far too heavy for the aerocycles to lift him off the ground completely, but with the pull of the ropes he managed to use his back legs to scramble up the cliff face. When he approached the lip of the cliff, Jackson felt the ropes give way suddenly and both his and Zeina's aerocycles leapt forward, sending them crashing to the ground. The blubber chamber broke away from Zeina's aerocycle and lay smashed in the snow.

'Ow!'

'What happened?' Jackson asked, rubbing snow from his bruised chin.

'He let go!' said Shrapnel.

And as they all picked themselves up and went over to the

cliff they could see the outline of the guard, using his great paws and the last of his strength to pull his back legs to safety. Katu grabbed him under one arm and Lotti under the other and together they hauled him up until at last all four paws rested on the ice plain.

The guard gave himself a shake, fluffing his dampened fur and sending out a spray of snowflakes in all directions. It was only when the guard stood upright, reaching his true magnificent height, shoulders broad, arms outstretched, and let out an almighty howling roar that Jackson recognised that he was not a guard at all.

That roar was the roar of the Emerald King.

CHAPTER 15

Zeina recoiled, frozen palms flying to her numb cheeks, as the Emerald King turned on Lotti with a shocking ferocity. Bent double and puffing from the effort of lifting him, his roar had caught Lotti by surprise. She fell backwards into the snow, her paws shielding her face from his mighty jaws.

'How *dare* you?!' His curved canines glinted in the moonlight. 'Traitor! Traitor to the Feln, Traitor to the Emerald Crown!'

He launched himself over her, one huge paw landing either side of her shoulders where she lay flinching in the snow.

'Not so brave now, without your pistol, are you?' he bellowed centimetres from Lotti's terrified face. His breath made clouds in the dark coldness of the night. The children were silent statues, frozen with horror.

'And *you!*' The king turned on Katu, rising up to tower over his head. 'Pretending to be allies, pretending you were

150

seeking an alliance, when really you had *this* planned all along!'

'What is he talking about, Katu?' Zeina shouted over the storm. The wind was howling and the snow beginning to bury her boots. Albi circled overhead, his urgent cawing rising above the noise of the wind. She could sense Sparks shivering next to her and reached out to draw her in close. Sparks grasped Zeina's hand in both of hers and her tiny spindle fingers felt as though they were made of ice.

'We must find shelter,' Katu said, staring evenly at the ferocious king. 'This storm will get worse before it gets better and none of us are strong enough to make it back to the palace by foot or paw – even you, Emerald King.'

The king roared again into the night, but Katu did not flinch. He stood slightly lopsided, his bandaged leg held just clear of the ground, but his amber eyes did not break contact with the king's.

'How far away are we now?' Katu asked the king. 'Only you know your lands well enough to find the entrance to the cave in this storm. These children – who have saved your life, need I remind you – will lose theirs if we stay here.'

The king turned his focus to the children, glaring at each of them in turn. Jackson winced, Sparks tucked herself behind Zeina's back and, much to Zeina's annoyance, Shrapnel stepped forward, getting between her and the king.

The king growled with frustration. 'Fine. But there will be no mercy for her,' he roared at Lotti. 'Or you, *cousin*. Once this storm passes, you are done for. My guards will be searching for us.'

He fell back on to all fours, looking more beast-like than ever.

'You,' he growled sharply to Shrapnel. 'Take this cape for that small one before she freezes to death.'

The king bristled as Shrapnel unclipped the cape from his shoulders and then set off through the storm, his paws leaving giant prints in the snow.

'Katu,' Jackson whispered, his brow furrowed and eyes dazed. 'What is going on?'

'There'll be time to explain once we're sheltered, Jackson,' replied Katu. And then he did something Zeina had never seen him do before – he fell forward to walk on his front paws and his unbandaged back leg. 'It's quicker in the snow,' he winced. 'Especially with my injury. Lotti, can you take Sparks?'

Sparks's tiny frame was beginning to shake violently. Shrapnel draped the cape around her and scooped her up to put her on Lotti's back.

Lotti turned her head to look at Sparks, who cuddled herself around Lotti's backpack, still shivering under the cape. 'Hold on tight, OK?'

152

Zeina retrieved her and Jackson's aerocycles from the snowdrift. Jackson's was relatively unscathed so he folded it up and placed it inside his backpack, but the force of the fall had snapped Zeina's in two. It would take a lot of fixing when they got home to the *Nightjar* – *if* they ever got home to the *Nightjar*.

They set off at a steady pace, Katu limping along behind the king with Zeina, Jackson and Shrapnel trudging behind him, and Lotti and Sparks at the rear. Albi flew ahead and then circled back, swooping low to check they were all still there. Zeina focused on the ground, her feet trying to find the gaps in the snow left by the king's great paws.

The snow fell in a curtain, obscuring the landscape around them. Jackson and Shrapnel crept in on either side of her for warmth and soon they were all walking in a tight huddle. There were so many questions in Zeina's head, but she was so cold and so tired and so hungry that she had to block everything else out. For a long time, it was just her watching her feet find footfalls in the snow, Jackson and Shrapnel shivering on either side of her.

And just when she felt sure she couldn't take another step, she heard Jackson's voice, shaky but hopeful. 'Zeina, we're nearly there, look!'

Zeina forced herself to look up from the ground and, sure

enough, just a few metres away was a great gaping entrance to a cave, giant stalactites hanging like teeth.

They sped up, reaching the welcome shelter from the storm.

Zeina wasn't sure how, but the Emerald King had managed to start a fire inside the cave. It was tiny to begin with, stuttering and smoking, but as the Emerald King busied himself, building it up with twigs and branches he had found within the cave, it grew bigger and brighter.

'Quick,' Katu said to the children. 'Take off your wet outer things and get round the fire. Zeina, help me with Sparks.'

Together, Katu and Zeina took the wet cape from Sparks and placed her next to the fire. She was so pale, blue fingers curled up against her white cheek, but as the flames radiated their warm orange glow, her shivering eased.

Lotti and Shrapnel worked together, using the ropes from the aerocycles to string up the wet clothes high above the warmth of the fire. Katu curled himself around Sparks, who snuggled into his fur. After setting up the clothesline, Lotti reached into her pack and presented them with a jar of pickled fish to pass around and a flagon of lilaberry juice that she placed in the fire to warm. The fish smelled awful, but Zeina was so hungry she gobbled down three from the jar. Katu fed his fish to Albi, who croaked gratefully and then flew up to find a nook near the roof of the cave. For a long time they all just sat around the fire, staring into the flames in silence.

It seemed that Shrapnel was the first to thaw out.

'So who is going to explain to us what in heavens is going on?' he said, his voice echoing in the silence of the cave.

'Ha,' replied the king. 'You will have to ask Lotti as *she* is the one who started all this. You have her to thank for the trouble you are all in now.'

Lotti snarled. 'How dare you? This is all down to *you*, King. You and your obsession with the Emerald Crystal and the Emerald Crown started all this, not me.'

'They belong to the Feln,' the king snapped back, the flames of their fire dancing in his eyes. 'Those filthy humans had no right to take them and keep them from us for so long. You have spied on your king and betrayed your own people.'

Lotti growled in disbelief and the king began to rise up, his black lips curling back to show his teeth.

'Calm yourselves,' Katu sighed. 'There is no point fighting each other while the storm rages outside. We have time to explain to these brave children, the events that have brought us here, before we decide what we are to do next.' He rose, reaching for the now-dry cape to drape over Sparks, who was looking much better. The warmth from the fire and fur had left rosy marks on her cheeks.

155

Katu took a seat and looked at them all in turn. 'First of all, Lotti here is my great-niece.'

Zeina stared at Lotti and suddenly a few things clicked into place. Lotti was much smaller than the other adult Feln she had seen at the palace and her markings were slightly darker. Now she realised that her fur seemed a mixture of Kotarth and Feln, as did her face. The way she frowned when she was concentrating in her workshop reminded her of the way Katu looked when he was examining a map, and yet her ears were rounder like the king's, rather than pointed like Katu's.

'Your great-niece!' Shrapnel laughed. 'How old *are* you, Katu?'

'Much older, and wiser, than you,' Katu growled teasingly.

'My grandad was Katu's brother,' Lotti explained. 'He visited here many decades ago and fell in love with my grandma, a Feln. I have always kept in touch with my Kotarth family and since Katu started working for the Smog Rats, I've been a contact for him here in the north.'

'A spy,' the king spat accusingly. 'A traitor!'

Lotti ignored him. 'When I heard the rumours about what the king had done to get back the Emerald Crown and the Emerald Crystal, I realised I would need to investigate. But I needed help. So I spread rumours around the palace about the Smog Rats' technology, planting the seed that we should invite them to the festival.'

The king had a look of utter disbelief at the realisation that he had been tricked.

'I knew Captain Parr was seeking an alliance with the king and thought it would also serve as a cover for me to investigate,' Katu explained. 'And since being here, we have confirmed that Lotti was *right* to be concerned.' His voice grew stern as he looked at the Emerald King, who seemed to shrink under his gaze.

'I have no idea what you're talking about. I only did what was best for my kingdom,' the king replied haughtily, resting his chin on his paw. 'The Emerald Crown and the Emerald Crystal are vital – they are our history.'

'If you believe you were right, you won't mind explaining your actions now, will you?' Katu insisted. 'Tell them!' Katu roared loudly when the king said nothing, louder than Zeina had ever heard him before.

'I do not take orders from you, cousin. But as I have nothing to be ashamed of . . . Many months ago, a human arrived in Palik,' the king began. 'He said he had come into the possession of some items that belonged to us and wanted to return them to the Feln, where they belonged. They were, of course, the Emerald Crown and the Emerald Crystal. Was I supposed to say no?' he demanded of Katu. 'Turn down the

157

chance to reclaim our national pride? Sacred treasure that was stolen from us long ago?'

'And what did you give him in return?' glared Katu.

The king's eyes darted around the cave. He lowered his voice, so quiet that Zeina could not hear what he was saying.

'Louder!' roared Katu.

'*Some land*, that is all. A plot of barren land just north of this mountain. Nothing of any consequence,' the king admitted.

'You broke your father's promise by opening our land up to airships,' Lotti hissed.

'Who was he?' Jackson demanded. 'What did he want with the land?' Jackson was flushed and quivering. Zeina suspected that he was wondering if this man could be his Uncle Hamilton.

'I don't know.' The king threw up his arms. 'Humans all look very similar to me – this one was small and skinny, a tiny human about the size of him.' He pointed to Shrapnel. 'But he had glasses, and a beard that was black rather than fair.'

Jackson sighed, seeming almost disappointed. No matter how bad the king was at describing humans, Hamilton was much taller and broader than Shrapnel and his hair was the same copper-brown as Jackson's.

'He said they needed a site to build airships, that's all; somewhere away from a rival company. They promised to take care of the land and return it to me after they had finished their project,' the king added. 'A good trade, I thought, for two *priceless* pieces of our history.'

'And you believed him,' Katu scoffed.

'He didn't care,' Lotti growled. 'As long as he got to wear that crown, bask in the glory of having the crystal atop his palace, he didn't care.'

'It was the right decision,' the king snarled, stubborn as ever. 'The jewels in exchange for the temporary use of a small plot of land? The airships will be gone eventually and yet the Feln have a new sense of pride and honour.'

The storm had settled and the moon peeped out from a clearing in the clouds. It seemed brighter outside the cave despite it now being close to midnight.

'I am not the traitor here. Let's not forget that the two of you have *kidnapped* me – the Emerald King – forced me out into a dangerous storm with a pistol pressed to my back, endangered my life.' The king stood up on his back legs, chin raised. 'My guards will be well aware of your deception by now, and there will be *severe* consequences indeed.'

'We will face those consequences later,' said Katu calmly. 'But first you will show us this land you have given away. We must find out what this human is really doing with it.'

'I will do no such thing!' the king scoffed. 'I am returning to my palace. I'll leave you here for my guards to deal with.'

'It will take you many hours to get back on foot,' said Lotti. 'And there are no Glindaskis for your guards. It could be days before they find us.'

'*You* smashed up the Glindaskis?' Zeina asked.

'I didn't want us followed,' Lotti explained with a sheepish shrug. 'Although it's a good job that didn't stop you lot!'

As Lotti smiled at her, Zeina realised how relieved she was that Lotti hadn't betrayed them. She could see how, in the darkness, Sparks could have mistaken the sight of Lotti holding a pistol and walking with a guard and the injured Katu as two Felns taking Katu hostage, instead of the other way around.

'Was it you who got rid of the ice ravens too?' Jackson asked.

'The ice ravens?' Lotti frowned. 'What do you mean? We took Albi but that's all.'

The king called across the cave to Katu. 'What are you doing?' he demanded.

Katu had called Albi down from his nook and was securing something to his foot, as he cawed and hopped around.

'Now the storm has passed, I am sending a message. Albi will take this to Nedra at the Glacial Palace and then on to

160

Captain Parr in Palik. I have explained everything and requested that the *Nightjar* come immediately once they receive the message. I should have told her straight away about Lotti's suspicions, but I first wanted proof – to see it with my own eyes. The time for that has passed. The *Nightjar* should be able to reach us by the time the sun rises.'

The king huffed, unfazed.

'Need I remind you that it is likely Pseudonym is among them?' Katu smiled, knowing this would rile up the king. Albi, his message now secured, began to stretch out his wings. 'I would guess your subjects will be *most* angry once they read all about this deal you have made in their favourite newspaper.'

'No! Stop!' The king staggered to his feet, desperately grasping in the air at Albi, who transformed into glitter and disappeared out of the cave's mouth. He roared after the bird and then turned to Katu. 'Whatever deal I've made is nothing for the Smog Rats to concern themselves with. If I decide to offer some land for an airship factory, that is none of your business.'

'You wouldn't mind Pseudonym seeing it then,' Katu smiled.

The king's ears flicked; his bushy fur had lost some of its magnificent splendour. He sat back on his haunches.

'What do you want?' he asked.

'Take us to the land and we can examine the true damage your decision has caused. We might even be able to clean up your mess before your subjects find out.'

'Fine,' he growled eventually through gritted teeth. 'And what about the children?' he asked, waving a paw over them as if they were luggage rather than actual beings.

'They will have to come with us,' Lotti said, looking around the fire at them all. 'You'll freeze on the way back if you're on foot. The human the king sold the land to must be using some form of transport. Maybe we can find an airship or sledge to get you back to the palace safely once we find out what is going on.'

Zeina nodded. There was no way she was being left behind in the cave while Lotti, Katu and the king found out about this mysterious human and the land he had bribed the king for.

'It seems you leave me no choice,' the king snarled.

'Excellent.' Katu smiled. 'Now, is there a way to get through this mountain using these caves rather than going back outside?'

'Yes,' the king sighed. 'If we follow the system, we should reach the other side of the mountain eventually. That is where the land in question is located.'

After quickly packing up their things and putting back on their dried outer clothes, the group set off. They followed the king, as before, but this time down into the twisting chamber of the cavern. And soon Zeina could hear the faint thrum of a familiar but unwelcome sound – the distant rhythmic clanking of heavy machinery.

CHAPTER 16

I t was pitch-black inside the mountain. The darkness didn't seem to faze the king, who kept up a steady padding, ducking under arches and weaving around huge stalagmites with ease. But the children needed to get their whale-blubber lamps working again in order to see where they were going.

'Remember, the Feln are accustomed to five months of darkness a year,' Lotti explained. 'We've adapted to have eyes that can see in very low levels of light.'

Lotti and Sparks rode out in front, Sparks holding a smoking lamp at arm's length. The stench of burning fat caught at the back of Jackson's throat but he was grateful for the lamp all the same. Twice they would have walked off the path and fallen into the bottomless depths of the mountain were it not for its glow highlighting the danger. The floor of the cavern was rough and rocky in places and covered in a smooth but lethal layer of crystal-blue ice in others. Jackson tried his best not to think about the metres of solid rock above his head.

Eventually the lighting began to improve. They had walked right through the mountain and were approaching the other side. Holes opened up in the rocks above them and shafts of moonlight made spotlights on the floor.

But as the light grew brighter, the eerie metallic clanking grew louder too. Soon the exit of the cave loomed in front of them and the king stopped, his ears cocked.

Through the opening they saw a stretch of greying ice plain, scattered with at least twenty moored airships of different sizes. The melting snow dripped off the ships, staining the ice ore-black and rust-red in places. Beyond them was another mountainside. A huge building had been built into it – steel girders with great glass windows – and behind that the motion of mining equipment working at full capacity.

The air was saturated with the clunk and rattle of machines and that toxic smell that served Jackson an unwelcome reminder of his home in Ravenport. Zeina gasped in horror.

'Is *this* what you agreed to?' Katu snarled at the king.

The king's black nose sniffed the air. 'It smells like an airship factory to me,' he confirmed, and yet his gaze narrowed on a queue of humans making their way from the moored airships to the grand entrance of the building.

It reminded Jackson a little of the line of Aboves that came to his annual birthday bash – aviator uniforms, bright suits and grand dresses all punctuated by the dark-green uniforms of lawkeepers. The only differences were the lack of children and the fact that many also wore big fur coats and tall furry hats to keep out the bitter northern chill.

'We need to know what's going on inside,' Jackson whispered. He hadn't seen many airship factories, but the site looked nothing like any airship factory he had seen before.

'We need to find a way in. If only we had a disguise,' said Zeina. 'Where's Nedra when you need her?'

So much had happened in the last few hours that Jackson had forgotten all about Nedra. He wondered whether she had been captured by the palace guards when it was discovered the king and the others were all missing.

'Even Nedra would find it hard to get past that lot.' Shrapnel pointed to the glass doors, where guards were checking that each little group had an invitation to go inside. 'You need a story for a disguise, and that's hard because we don't know who they are or what they're doing.'

'I know how to get us in unseen,' the king grumbled, almost reluctantly. 'That building has been built into an existing cave in the neighbouring mountain and there is a shaft that links that cave system to this. It is narrow and treacherous, but it would get us all in without having to walk across the plain.'

The king led them to the opening of the shaft, a steep tunnel coated in smooth ice. Katu stroked his beard. 'Climbing back up would be impossible,' he said. 'What happens if we get down there and then the opening is too narrow to get out?'

Sparks began to tug on Jackson's arm and he bent down so she could whisper into his ear.

Jackson explained her plan to the group. 'Sparks is volunteering to go down first.'

'Are you sure, Sparks?' Zeina asked.

She nodded and they all turned to Katu, who agreed.

They tied the two ropes together tightly; one end went around Sparks's middle and the other was tied around Lotti's.

'One tug on the rope means yes; two means no; tug three times when you're through,' Shrapnel said as he lifted her up.

Sparks gave a thumbs up before launching herself, disappearing into the shaft headfirst. The rope flew down with some speed before stopping with an icy thud.

'Sparks, are you OK?' called Zeina. There was a sharp tug on the rope and then it began moving again, this time at a slower speed. Just when they were about to run out of rope, Lotti felt three harsh tugs.

167

Zeina went next, a whoop of excitement echoing back up the tunnel as she slid down, and then it was Jackson's turn.

The tunnel seemed so narrow. What if he got stuck? He took a deep breath and pushed himself off, flying down the tunnel at great speed. Desperately, he tried to grip with his hands and feet to slow himself down, but the surface of the shaft was so icy and smooth that they would not catch.

'Ahhhhh!' His hands hit a boulder that jutted out and slowed him to a stop with a soft groan. He carefully edged himself around it, before sliding down the last part of the chute.

Eventually his head and shoulders popped out into another cavernous space and there, waiting to help him to the floor, were Zeina and Sparks.

'Fun, isn't it?' Zeina grinned.

Jackson wasn't so sure.

The next head to emerge was Shrapnel, followed by Katu and then the king. Jackson had wondered how the enormous king would fit down the narrow chute but noticed that he was curiously skinny underneath all his majestic fluffed-up fur. Last came Lotti with her backpack and the end of the rope.

In this cave, the sound of machinery was deafening and the smell of fumes almost unbearable. Katu whispered something to the king and then put one clawed finger to his lips to signal to the children that they must all remain silent from this point onwards.

The king set off on all fours, slinking cat-like down a narrow rocky path, where the noise became louder and louder. They followed, Lotti and Katu low and stealthy, the children staying close together in the shadows.

The path opened up into the vaulted ceiling of a rocky chamber and then formed a narrow ridge. They inched along the ridge and then crouched down to peer over the edge at the sight beneath them.

Jackson could see that they were now inside the very building they had seen across the plain. The chamber below was a cave in the mountain that had been transformed into something like an enormous theatre; the entrance was made up of steel and glass, there were rows of seats that the parade of people coming through the doors were beginning to fill, and near the back of the cave was a stage and lectern. Both the stage and seating area were brightly lit with gas lamps that thankfully threw the cavernous ceiling where they were hiding into shadow.

Above the noise from the machines rose the excited chatter of the guests below, each one clearly an Above from the appearance of their luxurious clothes and fine hats. Jackson scoured the gathering crowd for any sign of anyone he knew. He picked out many heads of prestigious Above families that he'd been introduced to at parties – the Penningtons, the Addlesmiths, the Silverfleets and the Tinkersons – but there was no sign of his Uncle Hamilton and he wasn't sure if this made him feel relieved or frustrated. Terrifyingly, there were also lawkeepers everywhere, lining the sides of the theatre and dispersed among the crowd.

The lights around the seating area dimmed and a hush went around the room. Katu, his eyes glinting from the shadows, placed a finger once again to his lips, reminding them to stay completely silent.

The lamps around the stage became dazzling as a small man walked towards the lectern, to a round of applause.

'Good evening,' he announced, his dark hair coiffed neatly and his thick, round glasses pushed up to the bridge of his nose. His grey eyes shone with excitement. 'Ladies and gentlemen, thank you so much for being here!'

He threw open his arms and smiled, his neat black beard bristling slightly in the glare of the stage lamps. There was something familiar about him, although Jackson couldn't place where he had seen him before. At a party back in Ravenport maybe?

The king stared down at this man and growled. Katu nudged him silently, and only then did Jackson remember the description of the human who had come to bribe the king for land. No wonder he seemed so familiar!

'Soon I shall introduce you to the head of our organisation, but first I would like you to meet someone who can tell you all about our new venture. We are expecting our services to be in high demand, so if you are interested make sure you express this to one of our staff as soon as possible. There will be time for you to ask questions individually later, so for now just sit back and join me in welcoming our top scientist, Dr Giles Mortwell, on to the stage.'

A tall man wearing a smart black lab coat buttoned right up to his neck strode on to the stage to the sound of more applause. His grey hair was parted down the middle into stiff waves that echoed the shape of his moustache.

Jackson was surprised to find he recognised the man. Though his hair had been black back then, he was unmistakeably the scientist Jackson had seen in photographs of his father and grandfather at their STANS facility many years ago. There was something nightmarish about him that made him unforgettable. His cold grey eyes stalked the room; the venomous sneer that twisted his lips sent a chill to Jackson's very core. He felt Sparks shudder next to him and saw that she was terrified, her breathing coming in little ragged gasps.

'Good evening,' Dr Mortwell said. His voice made Jackson feel like spiders were climbing his shoulders and crawling up the back his neck. 'Today marks the beginning of a new era.

An era in which we will put our petty rivalries behind us and share our information and technologies freely with one another. Recent times have been marred by the efforts of some to disrupt our way of life. By investing in what I am about to show you, you are investing in a better future, a safer future!'

More applause, even louder than before, rang around the room. Some men wearing top hats stood up at the back and cheered. Dr Mortwell smiled that sly, cold smile, which made Jackson squirm again.

'Jackson,' Zeina whispered, trying to grab his attention.

But Dr Mortwell was speaking again and Jackson was too focused on what he was saying to pay Zeina any attention.

'This new discovery will revolutionise how we protect our homes and our businesses, keeping our families and guests safe, and in no small way we must thank a very dear friend of mine . . .'

'Jackson!' Zeina hissed. But Jackson put a finger to his lips, trying desperately to focus on what Dr Mortwell was saying.

'. . . has been gracious enough to share his family's top-secret technology with the world at last. And it is this knowledge plus the efforts of all the scientists who have worked so hard these past few months . . .'

'Oh, Jackson. I'm so sorry.'

Jackson turned to see Zeina's hands fly up to her mouth and everything seemed to move in slow motion. He turned back to the lectern just as a huge black-and-white image was projected on to the wall behind the stage, and a man climbed up the steps to the front. For a second he was nothing but a silhouette in the bright light coming from the wooden projector box. Jackson stared in horror at the image, a black etching of a horned sky whale encased round the middle by a steel harness, the word 'OSIRIS' written in capitals across it. On the top of the harness was a glass dome, big enough to house the two determined lawkeepers who were driving the beast forward towards an airship, its two huge tusks piercing the hull.

The crowd in the room below gasped and then rose to their feet, stamping and clapping and cheering so loudly that at first you could not hear what the man was saying.

Then above the noise: 'Dear friends, thank you, thank you. You are too kind!'

Jackson's world began to spin. He was glad that Zeina had managed to edge right up to him, her arm wrapped around his shoulder, or else he might have toppled off the ridge in shock.

For that charming voice was indisputably the person who had killed his parents and plotted to kill Jackson himself. There he was, basking in the adoration of the crowd. His uncle, Hamilton Willoughby.

CHAPTER 17

The crowd below roared as Hamilton Willoughby waved and chortled. Zeina was taken back to that first time she had met him at Jackson's birthday party, before she knew the depths he would plumb to get his hands on Jackson's fortune, and the part *she* would have to play in those plans. He appeared thinner and older; his moustache drooped slightly and his luxurious ruby suit was somewhat baggy in places, but he lapped up the attention from his audience with just as much vigour as he had that day back in Ravenport.

'Yes, dear friends, it was my remarkable father – Clement Oswald Willoughby – who revolutionised the world when he invented the STAN system, allowing humans to explore the Upper Atmosphere in safety and luxury. Now it is *I* who will save our way of life by sharing this knowledge with the world!'

He held out his palms, drinking in the raucous applause.

'You are too kind – it is my duty to do anything in my power to protect our lives, and the lives of the innocent sky whales targeted by these brutish pirate attacks.' Hamilton scowled at the crowd with all the drama of an actor in his starring role. His balled-up fist hammered into his palm. 'We should *not* be forced to attach harpoons and weapons to our magnificent airships. There should be *no need* for every ship to have its own lawkeeper. They should be on our streets, monitoring the misguided Belows who wish to join these Smog Rats.' Hamilton's expression changed to one of woeful melancholy. He sniffed, placing one hand over his heart as the other dabbed at the corner of his eyes with a handkerchief. 'Ever since the death of my dear brother and sister-in-law, and my poor, brave nephew Jackson, and the attack on my beloved Willoughby Whale . . . I swore that I would bring the perpetrators to justice.'

Zeina felt Jackson trembling with rage. His lips were pursed as if it were taking every fibre of his being not to yell out.

Hamilton switched off his tears like a tap. 'Now, dear friends, with my assistance the noble scientists of Osiris, led by our own Dr Mortwell, have engineered the *perfect* solution to our Smog Rats problem!'

Hamilton held out his arms to welcome Dr Mortwell back to the lectern. The scientist leered as he clicked through a number of slides. 'The horned sky whale provides us with the perfect tool to protect our sky whale hotels. They are smaller and faster, can easily outfly any of the Smog Rats' airships, and of course they come equipped with their own natural weapons. Their tusks are made from one of the strongest materials in the world, sharp enough to penetrate through any thickness of metal.'

The Emerald King snarled from the shadows, his shoulders hunched and claws twitching, as if he would like to pounce on to the stage and rip out Dr Mortwell's throat. Katu whispered something into his ear to calm him.

'Famously stubborn and elusive, the horned sky whale has never been successfully fitted with a STAN system before.' Dr Mortwell paused and his smug sneer made Zeina's stomach lurch. 'That is, until now! If you would all like to turn round. May I present to you, the Osiris Whale!'

The crowd got to their feet and turned to face the glass front of the building, muttering and peering over one another's heads. The lights went out to squeals of excitement. Suddenly the room was dazzled by bright floodlights from outside, which flashed and then rotated, turning into the sky.

Blinded by the lights, Zeina lifted her arm to shield her eyes. She squinted, desperately trying to see and then instantly wished she hadn't. For flying just outside the glass entrance was a real, live horned sky whale, its middle encased in a metal harness with OSIRIS engraved in large letters on the side.

It flew forward and then high up in the air, before diving almost to meet the ground. It performed a loop-the-loop to the enraptured applause of the crowd. It swooped around and towards the glass front of the building, making some of the audience gasp and duck, but then turned sharply upwards just before its tusks made contact with the glass. The crowd laughed and cheered in delight.

It was much smaller than the baby whale the Smog Rats had rescued from Steele last year, about the size of an automobile. There was a small glass dome built into the harness near its head, but no driver. They must be controlling it remotely, Zeina thought. Its hide was a pale silver rather than steel grey, but its eyes were haunted by the same dark helplessness she had seen in the eyes of any sky whale controlled by the STAN system.

She turned away, looking to Jackson, whose eyes brimmed with angry tears. Beyond him was Shrapnel, solemn and silent, and Sparks, who was still trembling uncontrollably. Thankfully the floodlights were soon switched off, casting the outside – and the horror of the whale – back into darkness. The crowd below turned back to Dr Mortwell, erupting into applause.

'Thanks to this collaboration between Hamilton Willoughby and Osiris, we have been able to purchase this land and the ancient knowledge of the Feln to observe, capture and successfully test young whales with the system!' he announced. 'The specimen you have just seen is a young prototype, but it will quickly triple in size, eventually providing a cockpit for two drivers, an engine room and storage for extra weapons.'

The king clawed at the ground, making the ridge where they were hiding shake and grumble.

The man with the black beard and glasses stepped forward to take over from Dr Mortwell. It was strange, for Zeina was sure she had never seen the man before, and yet there was something so familiar about him.

'What an incredible demonstration, don't you all agree?' The audience erupted into cheers and applause once more. 'Now, you may be asking yourselves, what can I do to acquire one of these magnificent whales?' he said, grey eyes shining with excitement behind his small, round glasses. 'Well, here to answer your questions is someone you may not have been expecting, but who really needs no introduction. Our greatest surprise for you this evening, ladies and gentlemen, please join me in welcoming on to the stage the Founder and President of Osiris.'

On walked a lady dressed in a most magnificent jade

gown, the bodice embroidered with gold and the skirt in ruched layers of silk. A high-crowned hat decorated in emerald brooches and peacock feathers sat at an angle atop waves of auburn curls. The crowd was shocked into silence as she approached the lectern.

'Good evening, my friends,' her voice sang in the stunned stillness of the room. 'I am so delighted to be here this evening, for it has been far too long.' She smiled, her electric-green eyes amused by the crowd's astonishment. An angry red burn scar across her left cheek did nothing to detract from her beauty.

Zeina felt as though she had left her body completely, like she was watching herself in a dream. How could *she* be here?

The glamorous figure began to speak again. 'Yes, dear friends, it is I – Vivianne Steele. I know the world feared I was dead. I apologise for keeping you in the dark for so long, but there are spies everywhere and "being dead" has served me very well these last few months.'

It seemed that Zeina was not the only one in shock – Hamilton's mouth was agape, and he had turned quite pale.

'Secrecy has been of the *utmost* importance in setting up my wonderful new company, Osiris. An ancient world once named Osiris their god of resurrection. And, just like the name, I have been reborn,' she smiled. 'We must all act now if we are to claw back our way of life from the brink of death.

The number of Belows who join the Smog Rats rises daily, and it is time for us to fight back. No more will we live in fear. No more will they steal what we have all worked so hard for!'

As if the spell had suddenly broken, the audience erupted into the loudest round of applause yet. Zeina's heart hammered and her head spun, Vivianne swimming in and out of focus.

CHAPTER 18

Vivianne Steele threw her arms wide as the crowd rose to a standing ovation. A dazzling smile set her face alight; her eyes danced over her adoring crowd. It was all like a terrible dream.

The last time Jackson had seen those eyes they had been wide with fear as her airship, the *Raven*, fell from the sky. How had she ever managed to survive the wreckage? Jackson had watched the sky whale attack her airship, tear it in two. He'd watched the pieces fall into Howlingwood and ignite against the trees.

Jackson felt Zeina's fingers dig into his forearm and, though her face remained pale, her eyes smouldered with rage.

'Thank you, my friends!' Vivianne motioned the crowd to a hush.

As Vivianne reached out to grab the hand of the black-bearded man, Hamilton bristled. Jackson knew that he had always prided himself on being 'a very dear friend' of the famous Vivianne Steele and he would hate that he had been kept out of the loop.

'Injured but alive, I was smuggled out of the Forest of Howlingwood, past the Kotarth army and into the Western Mining Grounds. It was from there, with a little help,' she smiled at the black-bearded man, who gazed back into her eyes in awe, 'that I was able to set up Osiris, in secret, and plan my triumphant return from the dead!'

There were squeals of amusement and a cacophony of cheers.

'And now, dear friends, I need *you* to act. The *world* needs you to act. Everyone here tonight has the invitation to order your very own Osiris Whale for a special introductory price! Your investment guarantees that you will be among the first to own one. As a bonus you can even watch your very own horned sky whale being caught in a live whale hunt we will hold just a few hours from now.'

The investors gasped, turning to each other to whisper in excitement. *A whale hunt? Here?* Jackson thought back to that awful day on the *Raven* – he could not imagine why anyone would want to watch that.

He peered along the ridge at Katu and Lotti. Lotti's eyes were watery pools. Katu scowled down at the stage, one paw resting on top of the king's to remind him of restraint.

'Our scientists have engineered a very special way to interact with the whales. Using vibrations tuned to a specific frequency, they can call whales towards a specific location, making them easy to catch. The technology has just been activated, meaning that the whales are already on their way and the hunt can begin at sunrise! Our technology will guide the youngest whales away from their pods, through a specially engineered net and into our underground STANS facility, with not a drop of blood in sight! And those of you assembled here, the fortunate few, can watch the whole spectacle from our champagne viewing gallery on top of the mountain.'

Jackson saw Lotti turn on the king, growling something in the cover of the applause from below.

'Tonight you also have the opportunity to purchase shares in Osiris, which are sure to rise exponentially as soon as news of my return reaches the morning newspapers.' Vivianne placed a gloved hand to her neck, where a diamond necklace glittered. 'We do have some limitations on availability, so if you would like to invest I suggest that you make yourself known right away.'

Her laughter tinkled around the room as everyone rushed from their seats to the front of the stage, some wildly gesticulating with their arms and others holding up fans of cash to wave at her. Jackson was grateful when Sparks gave him an urgent nudge to move. He could not bear to watch Steele or Hamilton, or the baying crowd, a moment longer.

The king continued to lead the way slowly along the ridge in the theatre's ceiling. At the end there was another smaller chamber with tunnels running in two different directions and a small hole above, through which Jackson could see the night sky. The rowdy room below was much too busy to notice the movement of the little group high above them. Through the hole, the low moon winked at them, reminding Jackson that he had been up all night. His stomach growled and his mouth felt dry. The sight of that poor whale being tortured into performing had left a bitter tang in his mouth that he could not shift.

It felt to Jackson as though years had passed since he waved Parr off yesterday lunchtime. All the worries he had then about Nedra, Pseudonym and the alliance now paled into insignificance. The thought of Hamilton with that self-satisfied smile on his face made his insides burn with an anger so fierce he feared it might consume him.

One by one they pushed themselves through the hole and up on to the mountaintop. Jackson breathed in the brisk night air, freeing himself from the suffocating stuffiness of the room they had left behind. The moon kissed the mountaintops with its golden glow, dyeing the star-strewn

184

sky an inky violet. Now the storm clouds had completely cleared, Jackson could see the first flickerings of the Smara Ignis – a turquoise trail across the sky – and were it not for the awful spectacle he had just witnessed looping in his brain, he would have found it all quite breathtaking.

CHAPTER 19

By the time Zeina had helped Sparks and Jackson haul Shrapnel up through the hole, Lotti and the Emerald King were already embroiled in an argument. They circled each other, claws out, teeth bared. Katu was trying to get between them and reminding them both to 'please keep your voices down'.

'That's *my* technology they're using to catch the whales, isn't it? One of my echophone machines. *You* gave it to them, didn't you?' Lotti hissed and spat. 'How could you? You are supposed to protect the whales. That technology was designed only to help us minimise pain and bloodshed on our yearly hunt, and you sold it away for treasure.'

'The human was not satisfied with merely the land,' the king snarled back. 'He had both the Emerald Crown *and* our Emerald Crystal – it would have taken decades for us to save enough to buy them both back. He promised they would only use the technology to *observe* the whales.'

'You didn't believe that for a second,' Lotti growled. 'You might not have imagined that they would use it like this, but you know what humans do to sky whales, and you gave them my invention anyway.'

'There is no time for this!' Katu roared so fiercely that they both stopped. 'Look down there,' he said, pointing to the far side of the mountain.

In the valley below, a giant net made of steel cables sparkled in the milky moonlight. Shaped into an enormous funnel, its mouth gaped into the night, ready to consume. It swooped along the valley and down into a wide hole underground. 'At sunrise that net will ensnare young horned sky whales, lure them down into the underground STANS facility, where each one will be tortured and turned into weapons that will destroy us.'

Zeina was certain she had never seen Katu so angry.

'Your actions, King, whether you meant it or not, have put the whole world in danger and now it is our job to fix it.'

'I must return to my palace,' the king growled, his head bowed. 'My guards will take back this land and kill anyone who tries to stop them.'

'There is no time,' Katu spat. 'Even if we steal an airship, by the time your guards arrive it will be too late. We will have to beat them with stealth rather than force. No one yet knows we are here, and that is our *only* advantage.'

'What can we do, Katu?' Shrapnel asked.

'We have three hours before the sun rises,' Katu replied, looking at his pocket watch. 'We must free that whale, destroy their STANS facility, get rid of all those investors and stop Steele from using Lotti's technology to capture any more young whales.'

Shrapnel scoffed. 'Oh yeah, sounds easy!'

'I never said it would be easy, but we have no choice. Albi will have delivered that message to the *Nightjar* by now and they will be on their way to find us. Do *you* want to see what will happen if they arrive and come face to face with that prototype whale under Steele's control? Plus all those Above airships and their harpoons? Even if we made it out alive, how do you think we'll fare six months from now, once every Above family has their own Osiris Whale?'

Shrapnel gulped.

'Come on then, Katu,' Zeina said. 'Just tell us what to do and we'll do it.'

He was silent for a moment, and Zeina could almost see the gears turning in his head.

'OK, we need a team to sneak inside the mountain and free the baby whale from the underground STANS facility. I have an idea for a diversion. It should draw most of the guards away. King, you will be best placed to communicate with the whale and keep it calm while the harness is removed.'

The king nodded solemnly. 'I owe the poor beast that at least,' he whispered.

'We need someone to take the STAN system off without harming the whale – someone who is familiar with it,' Katu continued.

'Sparks, weren't you rescued from a STANS room—' Shrapnel stopped when he saw the look on Sparks's face. She began to tremble again, shaking her head frantically and curling up into a little ball.

Zeina bent down, placing a hand on Sparks's back. She was quivering all over, her ice-white hands balled up in front of her mouth. Zeina could only imagine what horrors she had seen during her time in the Willoughby STANS facility – it was no wonder she didn't want to go anywhere near one. Jackson came in close, frowning with concern.

'It's all right, Sparks. You don't have to do anything you don't want to.'

She looked up at them both, her eyes bulging. 'I've met Dr Mortwell before . . . He's evil,' she whispered. 'Please don't make . . . I can't—' She broke off with a sob, unable to say any more.

'Dr Mortwell is infamously merciless,' Katu growled. 'He will let nothing get in the way of his research. He doesn't care about the pain it inflicts on other beings – in fact, some say he enjoys *that* most of all. Whoever goes with the king must get into the facility, rescue the whale and then get back out again as quickly as possible.'

Jackson stood. 'I'll go,' he said, his voice wavering slightly. 'Jamie has told me about the STAN system and shown me diagrams of how it attaches to the whale. I should be able to take it off. It's my family's invention, after all. Like the king said, it's the least I can do.' He rose to his fullest height, trying to convince the others – and himself – that he was up to the job. This was his chance to really help the whales. Zeina felt proud that her friend, once so scared and unsure of everything, would put himself forward for such a task.

'I'll come too,' Shrapnel said. 'I've been on enough whale raids that I should have picked something up by now!'

Katu stroked his bearded chin and nodded. 'Lotti, Zeina and Sparks, it's up to you to examine the net, find out exactly where the echophone technology is transmitting from and shut it down.'

They all nodded, Zeina helping Sparks to her feet. 'Come on, Sparks. They'll be running the whole thing off the electricity generated from that mine, and you know you're better at wires and circuits than anyone.'

Zeina flashed her a comforting smile and Sparks's trembling eased slightly.

'What about all the Above airships?' Zeina asked, looking down at the ice plain where they were moored. She could see that at least half of them had dart guns or harpoons fitted to the front and remembered the green lawkeeper uniforms scattered among the crowd. If the *Nightjar* arrived now, it would be like they had lured them into a trap. She thought about the last time she had seen her dad, less than twenty-four hours ago and yet it seemed like a lifetime. She could not stand the thought of him, nor any of her friends on the *Nightjar*, being injured in a battle where they were outnumbered and unprepared.

'Don't you worry about those, Zeina.' Katu's eyes glinted slyly. 'These investors will already be feeling a little skittish, being this far north, and I have much experience in causing chaos from the shadows.'

CHAPTER 20

'Be careful,' Zeina said, pulling Jackson into one of her tightest hugs.

'You too,' he said.

'And, whatever happens, don't get distracted by Hamilton.' She glared at him, like she could read his mind. 'He isn't worth it. Just rescue the whale and get out safely.'

Jackson nodded.

Already he was wondering what would happen if he encountered his uncle somewhere inside the facility. The simmering fury he had felt for months began to bubble when Jackson imagined confronting him, but he knew he would have to control himself if they were to make it in and out of the facility without being caught.

Zeina took hold of Jackson's hand in one of hers, and Shrapnel's hand in the other, giving them a squeeze. 'You look after each other, OK?'

'I'll look after him, Zee, don't you worry,' Shrapnel grinned, ruffling Jackson's hair, much to his annoyance. Shrapnel laughed as he batted him away.

The two boys waved a final goodbye to Zeina, Sparks and Lotti before following Katu and the Emerald King down through the hole and back into the mountain. The clamour of bartering investors still echoed from the presentation room.

'*Ten thousand, but I demand that the Silversmith family be the first to own one!*'

'*I will pledge thirty thousand, but I would like a matching pair.*'

'*What guarantees do you offer? If the tusks break, can I return it?*'

'*Do they come in a range of colours? I should like mine to match my airship!*'

That same bitter tang flooded Jackson's mouth. His stomach lurched and he felt warm and sticky despite the coolness of the dank, craggy chamber. Closing his eyes, he took in a few last, deep breaths of cool outside air from the hole above his head.

'Which way for an exit near the mine?' Katu asked the king.

'That tunnel there.' The king gestured with a large paw. 'Follow it down into the next chamber and then take the tunnel on the left. It comes out on the far north-east side. *We* must take this one to the west if we are to find an entrance into that underground STANS facility.'

Katu nodded. 'Here, Shrapnel, take my skeleton key. I think you're more likely to need it than I.' He handed him a long slender key of silvery white. 'Good luck,' he added, before disappearing in a flash of tail and whiskers.

Their tunnel was steep and uneven. It zigzagged down, opening into wide chambers and lofty caverns but was also so narrow in places that Jackson had to slide sideways like a crab or crawl along on his knees. Shrapnel held out the lamp in front of them and every so often a whiff of burning blubber would catch in Jackson's throat. He stifled his coughs, not wanting to be overheard or – worse – cause a rockslide.

Soon Jackson had lost all sense of where they were or which direction they were heading in. He hoped that the king knew his way, as without him he was quite sure they would be lost inside the labyrinth of twisted tunnels for ever.

At last the passage led them into a cave with some signs of life. Stacked up against the rough stone wall were a range of supplies – shovels, ropes, boxes of tools, sheets of metal, barrels of fish guts and crates of ore. The king motioned for them to duck behind one of the crates.

'There's an entrance to a large cave just around that bend,' he whispered. 'From the position of that net on the outside, it must be where they are keeping the whale. It's the only cave in the system that would be large enough.'

Jackson went to peer round the crate but was stopped by Shrapnel.

'If there's a guard there, he'll see you,' Shrapnel whispered. 'Here, let wise old Shrapnel show you a little spying trick I've learned in all my years of experience.'

Jackson rolled his eyes but was impressed all the same when, from his pocket, Shrapnel got out a little gold compact mirror that had been soldered on to an extendable metal stick. He positioned it in such a way that they could see round the corner without moving from their hiding place.

In the circle of mirror, they saw that a metal door, locked and bolted, had been set into the cave's wall. Two guards were chatting in hushed tones on either side, making it clear that Katu hadn't yet been able to cause a diversion.

'I could take them out in a swipe of my claws,' the king growled menacingly.

'You'd draw every lawkeeper in the place to us in a matter of minutes too,' Shrapnel hissed. 'Let's give it a minute. Katu won't let us down.'

Sure enough, just a few moments later, the air was filled with the blare of alarms, and the guards' radios began to crackle to life.

'All lawkeepers must report to the mine immediately. REPEAT. All lawkeepers *must* report to the mine immediately. Large fire in progress.'

'Told you!' Shrapnel grinned as they watched the guards hurry away.

They crept towards the door, which was tall and made of steel with a small, high hatch. Shrapnel took out Katu's skeleton key, which slid easily into each of the three locks, turning them one by one. The door creaked open and they sneaked inside, closing the door carefully behind them.

The underground STANS facility was dimly lit and it took Jackson a second or two to work out exactly what he was seeing. On one side there were tall machines, alight with dials and buttons. The strange low buzzing they emitted made all the hairs on the back of Jackson's neck stand to attention. In the centre an enormous net, shaped into a sort of chute, sloped down from the cave's ceiling where a circular hole, large enough for a young horned sky whale, had been excavated. It was barred by steel-toothed shutters.

Arranged in rows were at least twenty giant metal cages on wheels – ready for the hunt, Jackson supposed, and enough so that each of the investors upstairs could have their own whale. It looked as though each cage could be attached to the opening of the chute, for they all had the same ring of jagged metal teeth. The darkest recess of the cave was sectioned off from roof to floor by the same thick metal mesh that made up the net. There was a large hatch on one side, more jagged metal teeth and a control panel secured to the rocky wall nearby.

As they approached the darkness, it was the king who spotted the whale first. He held out a paw for them to stop, his eyes alight with sorrow.

'It is afraid,' he whispered. 'It can't attack, not with its STAN system attached. But it is terrified. Move slowly; we don't want to scare it any more than it is already.'

Behind the net, the whale hovered in mid-air. Its tail undulated up and down, its two great tusks swaying slightly with the motion of its tail, but it did not move forwards or backwards an inch. It was as if someone had put it on pause. On the whale's steel harness, the letters 'OSIRIS' glinted at Jackson from the gloom. The whale's hide was the same silvery white as its magnificent tusks that twirled out from its nose into two razor-sharp points.

'We'd better get a move on,' said Shrapnel.

'I agree,' grumbled the king. 'You see if you can get that hatch open. Young Jackson and I will go in.'

'Go *inside* the net?' Jackson exclaimed, panic rising in his chest.

'I don't see how else you're going to get that thing off, do you?' growled the king. 'Don't worry, I should be able to keep it calm.'

On his way to the control panel, Shrapnel paused to look up at the chute. 'The exit is blocked,' he said. 'After I open the hatch, I'll have to see about getting those shutters open as well, or else the whale will be trapped inside here with us.'

'Yes,' agreed the king. 'The whale needs to be able to fly out of this cave as soon as the STAN system is removed. Otherwise it could panic and kill us all.'

Jackson gulped.

Shrapnel busied himself at the control panel and the hatch opened. The king went up to the whale first and placed one of his paws gently on top of its nose. Its murky eye blinked and then seemed to refocus with a new intensity on the king.

'Come on then, boy,' the king said in a growling whisper. 'Get on with it.'

Jackson took a deep breath and walked through the hatch. The steel harness was fitted tightly, cutting into the whale's hide and causing painful-looking ridges on either side. There was an enormous hinge on one side and a bolt on the other.

Since discovering the true horror of his family's invention, Jackson had decided to find out as much as possible about the STAN system. Jamie was the resident expert aboard the *Nightjar* and over the last few months he had patiently shown

Jackson diagrams and drawings so he could learn how it worked, and, more importantly, how it could be stopped.

Jackson thought back to all those diagrams now, but the harness in front of him looked completely different. He supposed, whatever happened next, the first thing he had to do was to get that bolt open.

'Shrapnel, find something like a hammer, can you?'

Shrapnel hunted around and then passed a toolbox through the hatch.

With a little effort the bolt soon clanked to the floor, startling the whale, whose tail began to swish faster and faster.

'Ssshh, it's OK, little one,' Jackson hushed, the gruff but gentle voice of Jamie playing in his head. He stroked the whale's head a little, which seemed to calm it down.

'This comes naturally to you, boy,' the king muttered. 'I can tell this whale trusts you. Don't let it down, OK?'

Jackson managed to take apart the hinge and release the bottom half of the metal harness. It hit the floor with a heavy clunk. Jackson grimaced. The hide underneath was tinged red and covered with painful-looking cracks and sores.

'Poor thing,' he sniffed. If he thought too much about what the whale had been through, what would happen if their plan failed, he knew it would consume him. Right now, he had to focus on the task at hand.

All that remained was the half of the harness that encircled the whale's head, but that was where the STANS mechanism would be located, connected somehow to the whale's brain. Jackson had to be careful. In the diagrams Jamie had shown him, the STANS room of a sky whale hotel had a whole unit with a network of wires that plugged into the whale's nervous system. By destroying the unit, they freed the whale from its control. Jackson was looking for something like that but on a *much* smaller scale. He gently prised the top of the harness away from the underlying hide, running his hand over the smooth of the whale's back. It lurched in pain.

'I'm sorry. Just a little longer,' Jackson hushed. He walked towards the whale's head, moving his hand under the harness. A mechanical whirring somewhere beyond the cave made Jackson freeze. A shaft of moonlight came from somewhere above the chute, shining through the net and covering the floor of the cave in a criss-cross pattern of shadows.

'The shutters are open!' Shrapnel exclaimed.

'How much longer, boy?' The king grimaced. Both his large paws were settled on the whale's nose. The king's eyes were clenched shut, his black nostrils flared and the fur on his neck stood up. 'He's getting more and more agitated.'

'I think I'm nearly there,' Jackson replied.

'I'm going to take a quick peek outside,' Shrapnel said. 'Make sure the coast is clear for *our* exit too.'

Jackson heard the door creak open and then click closed. He focused back on the whale, pushing all thoughts of Hamilton, Steele and lawkeepers aside as best he could.

At last he felt it! A little bundle of wires running on the underside of the harness and into a small hole in the hide behind the whale's eyes, just underneath where the glass dome was positioned.

He heard the door of the room swing open again and then close with a soft click.

'Shrapnel, I've found it!' Jackson whispered. 'Come and get the wire cutters for me, will you? I can't quite reach.'

'I don't think that will be necessary,' a sinister voice rasped from the gloom. Jackson turned his head, his hand still clutching the little bundle of wires. Terror gripped him like a vice as the dark figure snaked into the light. The king roared, launching himself at the hatch door as it swung to a heavy close. Without the king's comfort, the whale began to buck. Its nose, with its razor-sharp tusks, swung desperately from side to side, missing the king's head by mere centimetres. Though his feet were raised off the ground, Jackson held on to the wire bundle as tightly as he could. His free hand hunted urgently for any tool he might use to sever them.

'I wouldn't do that if I were you. The moment you destroy the STANS mechanism, the whale will panic, trapped in that small space, and it will turn on you,' said Dr Mortwell, pressing buttons on one of the tall machines near the door. Lights positioned near the whale's head flickered on and what was left of the harness began to hum and buzz. Lit by the dials of his machine, a malevolent smile played about the doctor's lips. It made Jackson feel as if he had been dunked beneath the surface of an icy lake. 'Now,' he said, 'step away from my whale.'

CHAPTER 21

Z eina watched Katu nod a solemn goodbye and disappear back inside the cavernous system. On all fours, his injured leg didn't seem to be bothering him too much, and yet Zeina still worried it might give him away – she knew only too well that drawing the attention of the lawkeepers was likely to be the most dangerous part of their plan. Watching Shrapnel and Jackson as they followed the king back into the hole, Zeina was struck by how small they both looked in comparison to his great size. She waved, her smile flickering as she tried to shake away a heaviness in her chest.

Then it was their turn to begin their mission down the steep rocky mountainside towards the valley where the giant tunnel of metal netting lay in wait for its prey. Feeling exposed and fearing someone may spot their lamps, Zeina, Sparks and Lotti did their best to find safe footholds down the mountain, using only the light of the moon. Lotti went first, her paws much better adapted to creeping down icy mountainsides. Once or twice Zeina or Sparks would slide on a patch of crystal ice, sending a deluge of snow and earth down the slope and they would all have to duck down behind one of the conifers that clung to the rocks, terrified that they had been heard.

When they reached the valley, the net was quite unguarded.

'Maybe Katu has already worked his magic?' Zeina suggested.

'Could be,' Lotti nodded. 'Or perhaps all the lawkeepers were needed inside for crowd control. They still don't know we're here, remember. They don't know that anyone is going to try and stop them.'

The tunnel was constructed from a thick net of woven metal cables. It opened upwards into the sky and then swooped along the valley and down, disappearing into an enormous hole in the valley floor.

'That will lead straight to the STANS facility, I would think,' Lotti hissed.

Zeina stood on the very edge and was gripped with a sudden nausea as the dark hole loomed ominously back at her. The facility must be buried deep underground. There was no way a human could reach it from this valley – it was a sheer drop of at least ten metres, and then two great metal jaws were clamped tightly shut across its exit. Zeina hoped that Shrapnel, Jackson and the king were already down there somewhere and hadn't come into contact with any lawkeepers along the way. Sparks joined her, peering down over the precipice, and shuddered.

'Come on,' Zeina whispered, placing an arm around Sparks's tiny shoulders. 'We need to find where they are transmitting the signal from.'

Lotti stood up on her hind legs, closed her eyes and listened, just like Katu did when he was tracking sky whales. Her black-tipped ears cocked and then flattened, flinching like she was in pain. Her tail bristled.

'It's horrible,' she choked. 'They've adjusted the whale song to speak directly to the youngest whales. It feels bright and happy, beckoning them into their trap.'

'Won't the adult whales follow them?' Zeina frowned.

'They will,' said Lotti. 'But they won't see the danger until it's too late. An adult horned sky whale won't fit inside that net. And then there are always *those* to scare them away if needed.' Lotti's eyes tracked up the opposite side of the valley, where, silhouetted against the light of the moon, there were three deadly-sharp harpoon guns.

'Come on,' Lotti muttered, dropping back on to all fours. 'We are far too exposed here. The signal is coming from up there.' Her dappled nose pointed to a place just above the

205

harpoon guns, where a thicket of trees grew thickly around a rocky outcrop.

The stars grew fainter. Zeina looked at her watch and saw that an hour had already gone by; that meant there were now only two until the sun rose. She sped up, forcing her aching legs to climb faster. They crept past the towering harpoon guns, their jagged spearheads cutting into the sky but thankfully abandoned – for now.

When they neared the thicket, Lotti's ears pricked up. She sank low to the ground and beckoned for Zeina and Sparks to do the same, crouching behind the trunk of a spruce. The sound of voices drifted through the branches. Lawkeepers, at least two of them.

'It gives me the creeps,' Zeina heard one of them say. He sounded no older than herself or Jackson.

'Well, if it stops the pirate attacks, it's all for the greater good,' an older voice replied.

'You won't catch me driving one, that's for sure,' the younger voice scoffed. 'I don't trust it.'

'You'll do exactly as you're told, if you know what's good for you!' the older man replied. 'We're a way off from revolution yet, no matter what that *Smog* paper says. Anyway, I doubt those in charge will be trusting *you* with a horned sky whale anytime soon. You can barely hold a pistol! Why do you think we've been placed out here? I'm too old and you're too young to be anywhere near the action.'

'Will there *be* any action tonight?' the younger lawkeeper asked, his voice wavering slightly.

'Nah, shouldn't think so. The Smog Rats won't be expecting any of this – they've kept it all top secret, haven't they? Even we didn't know anything about it until an hour or two ago.'

Zeina peered around the lower branches of the tree, making out the two dark figures between the forest of trunks. Lotti placed a clawed finger to her lips and then motioned for Zeina and Sparks to stay where they were. She slunk ahead, tree to tree, silently getting closer and closer to the pair.

'Here they come, look up there!' the younger voice exclaimed, reminding Zeina of an excited child rather than a lawkeeper.

'So they are,' the older voice replied. 'Well, I never! This thing must be doing something right, I guess.'

Zeina and Sparks looked up into the sky and there they were – horned sky whales – shadows against the violet sky. They dived and swooped a happy dance. For a moment Zeina was mesmerised but then, remembering why they were there, her chest filled with a sickening dread – they *had* to get to that machine.

Lotti was very close to the pair now, her head close to the ground, front legs bent, tail lashing. What was she about to do? The young lawkeeper had stood up and moved a little in the clearing, staring up in wonderment at the sky whales. Was Lotti about to attack him? She had no pistol but her teeth and claws were every bit as sharp as the king's. Suddenly Zeina was gripped with the urge to yell out and warn him. She clapped her hands around her mouth. Lotti sank lower, a spring ready to pounce.

A crackle of a radio broke the silence.

'All lawkeepers must report to the mine immediately. REPEAT. All lawkeepers must report to the mine immediately. Large fire in progress.'

'Fire?' the younger lawkeeper gasped, the spell of the sky whales broken.

'Come on,' the older one said, groaning as he got to his feet. 'I was in the mining grounds myself once upon a time – fires are pretty common. They'll want it out quickly though. Won't want it to scare off the investors, I'd imagine.'

The lawkeepers stumbled away from the clearing and, once she was sure they had gone, Zeina stood up. She and Sparks made their way to Lotti, who was watching the huge metal trumpet of the machine. It was at least ten times the size of the one Zeina had seen in Lotti's workshop.

The effect on her was obvious – Lotti's eyes had become sharp crescents and her nose wrinkled, her upper lip bared to reveal a snarl. Yet Zeina could not hear a thing.

'What were you going to do to those lawkeepers if they hadn't got that call?' Zeina couldn't help but ask.

'I would have done what I had to do,' Lotti replied, taking Zeina aback with the ferocity of her growl. 'Sorry,' she continued, her glare softening. 'It's this noise. I can't stand to listen to it a moment longer! They've amplified it,' she added, reaching out to tap the giant horn. 'It'll be calling whale pods from all over the Northern Continent. They'll hear it from hundreds of miles away.'

She took off her backpack and handed it to Sparks.

'We've got to move fast,' she whispered. 'Sparks, find us some screwdrivers so Zeina and I can get these panels off and take a look at the mechanism underneath. Then you can help me with the wires inside.' She glanced up into the sky at the whale-shaped shadows, growing larger and larger. 'We need to hurry!'

CHAPTER 22

Dr Mortwell picked up a small metal device from one of his machines. It was shaped in such a way that the scientist could easily hold it in two hands and operate the levers and buttons while watching a row of moving dials. The whale responded as if under a spell – its eyes returning to their glassy stare. Looping up in a tight, controlled circle, the creature rounded on the Emerald King from above. The king roared, gnashing at the hatch with his jaws, his claws gripping the net. The entire thing shook and rattled, sending debris from the cave ceiling to the floor, but the hatch refused to open.

Jackson backed against the wall of the cave, getting as far from the king and the whale as he could. The whale paused in mid-air, the tips of its tusks just centimetres from the king's head.

'Now, Emerald King, fancy meeting *you* here!' Dr Mortwell said, smirking. 'You know better than anyone what these tusks can do. Get right back into the corner with the boy, before I decide to give him a demonstration.'

Jackson was relieved when, with a final bloodthirsty howl, the king backed away from the hatch.

'Good,' the doctor responded. 'Now, let me see. *Who* exactly do we have here?' He moved towards the net, taking a pair of silver spectacles from his top pocket. 'Come a little closer, young man. I can't see you back there in the gloom.'

Jackson crept forward, his eyes darting to the whale's horns. He watched the doctor's grey eyebrows bristle behind his spectacles then raise in surprise. Dr Mortwell grinned, thin lips and two rows of neat, sharp little teeth appearing from underneath the curve of his moustache.

'Oh my, Jackson Willoughby! I worked enough years with your grandfather to recognise his *double* when I see him. Steele isn't the only one to have returned from the dead this evening, I see!' he cackled. 'I'm certain your Uncle Hamilton won't be quite as glad to see *you*. Seems much of what the papers reported last year about that infamous whale hunt was untrue!'

He stroked his chin thoughtfully, and then turned his attention back to the king, who growled from the shadows. 'And Emerald King! What a surprise! As you can see, we have put the land and technology you gifted us to great use. Are you enjoying having your emeralds back?'

The king howled as if he had been kicked. 'You have no honour, none of you! You lied to me,' he snarled.

'Yes,' the scientist replied. 'Although the way it was told to me, you didn't ask too many questions either.'

The sound of the door opening made Jackson jump – he hoped that Shrapnel had the sense to hide somewhere rather than try to rescue them alone.

But he needn't have feared.

'Ah, Hamilton!' Dr Mortwell smiled. 'I have quite the *surprise* for you!'

Jackson felt a surge in his chest.

'Surprise?' his uncle's voice echoed in the rocky chamber. 'I think there have been *quite* enough of those this evening, Mortwell! What in the *skies* is going on? The alarms, the fire! And where has Steele disappeared to now? There's only so long I can keep the investors . . .'

His words trailed off as his gaze landed on the Emerald King and then, finally, his nephew.

'Jackson?' His voice wavered as he edged ever so slightly closer. 'But you're—'

'Dead?' Jackson finished, fury seething through his veins. 'Imprisoned in the mining grounds?'

'Oh, Jackson.' Hamilton's eyes darted nervously around the cave, taking in the horned sky whale, the growling Feln king. He cleared his throat. 'H-How miraculous! What a . . . a

212

relief!' He smiled widely, arms outstretched in welcome, but his eyes betrayed his panic.

Dr Mortwell laughed. 'You're not convincing anyone, I'm afraid, Hamilton. Better just be straight with the boy.'

'You killed my parents,' Jackson said, much more calmly than he felt.

'Oh . . . No! No! How could you say . . . Of course I didn't! They died in an *accident*, dear boy . . . You've been through so much – you're clearly confused!'

'You killed my parents – your own *brother* – and then you arranged for Steele to get rid of me and Zeina. Killed or lost to the mining grounds, wasn't it? You didn't care which, just so long as I was gone and you could claim the Willoughby fortune.'

Hamilton was as pale as snow, gibbering and muttering. 'Who? . . . Oh, the *Below* girl . . . No! . . . It didn't happen *quite* like that. You see—'

Dr Mortwell erupted into an evil cackle. 'This is delightful! Who knew this evening would be so entertaining?'

Jackson continued, everything he had thought since he had last seen Hamilton spilling out. 'You planned to use Zeina as a scapegoat, didn't you? She would have been dumped in the mining grounds too, if it wasn't for the Smog Rats.' Jackson could feel his anger beginning to boil. Hamilton

213

cared so little for anyone but himself that he had forgotten Zeina's name.

'No, Jackson, you misunderstand. You see, I just—' He sighed, as if he were explaining something very complicated to a child. 'Everything I did was for the sake of the family.'

Jackson saw red; the flames inside him surged. *How dare he?* Jackson roared, launching himself at the net which separated him from his uncle with such ferocity that Hamilton recoiled in shock. He stumbled backwards into Dr Mortwell, who fell to the floor, the metal device skidding away from his hands. The king took this as his chance, running at the net shoulder-first, putting all his weight against its strength. It stretched and buckled. Rocks from around the steel bolts that secured the net to the cave's ceiling began to fall. The king galloped back to the cave wall, preparing once again to charge the net.

'ENOUGH!' Dr Mortwell's voice cut through the chaos. He had the device that controlled the whale back in his hands. The whale woke, zooming towards the king with tremendous speed.

'No!' Jackson called out, stepping away from the net and raising both his hands in surrender. 'Stop! Don't!'

But the whale did not stop this time. It drove straight at the cavern wall where the king stood, its two tusks piercing the rock as if it were butter. The king was pinned, trapped tightly between the whale's horns, blood dripping from a

214

deep gash on his shoulder dyeing his soft white fur red. He roared and struggled but could not move.

'We've had our fun but there's no time for this,' said Dr Mortwell. He regained his composure, dusting off his black lab coat and stroking his moustache back into its sleek waves. He examined a pocket watch. 'Now, Hamilton, there is no reason why the hunt can't continue as planned. Are the investors on the viewing platform?'

Hamilton nodded.

'Good,' said the doctor. 'Despite your nephew's impressive efforts, the prototype whale is still in good working order. I can repair the harness easily and the net is intact. The fire in the mine will soon be out – some kind of distraction, I presume?' He raised an eyebrow at Jackson, ushering the question away with the flick of his hand when Jackson remained silent. 'No matter! The lawkeepers can easily round up any accomplices inside the facility. I will send a team of lawkeepers to check on our transmission device too.'

Jackson did his best not to flinch. He hoped Zeina, Sparks and Lotti had already completed their part of the plan and got away, and that Katu and Shrapnel were hiding somewhere safe.

'The young whales will be gathering as we speak,' Dr Mortwell continued. 'I must prepare this facility for the hunt and *you*, Hamilton, must return to what you do best – charming the investors.'

Hamilton nodded once again, straightening his hat and smoothing out the ends of his moustache.

'Now, is there any reason why I can't kill these two?' The doctor asked this breezily, as if he were asking Hamilton if he would like a cup of tea and a slice of cake, rather than if he were allowed to murder his nephew.

'Uncle,' Jackson said. 'You *don't* have to do this. I don't want the money or Willoughby Towers. I don't care about any of it. I just want you to stop. The STAN system is evil and you know it. There's plenty of other ways you could make money without doing *this*.'

'I . . .' Hamilton wavered, focus jerking from Jackson to the injured king to Dr Mortwell and then back again to Jackson. His dark eyes bore into Jackson's then became still and sure. 'No,' he said in a voice suddenly as hard as stone. 'There's no reason. Kill them both. And kill any accomplices the lawkeepers find too.'

Jackson screamed in anger as Hamilton turned on his heels in a swish of velvet coat-tails. Dr Mortwell beamed in villainous delight and began to move the levers and buttons on the metal device.

But just as the whale began to move away from the wall, the king now released from its tusks and slumping down towards the floor, there was an almighty bang from somewhere above. All the lights in the lab began to flicker. The buttons on the row of machines began to blink, dials moving side to side. Pistol fire rang from outside and then, muffled through layers of rock, the sound of screams echoed.

CHAPTER 23

'How much longer?' Zeina asked, passing Lotti the tools she asked for one by one. Sparks lay on her front on the cold ground, fiddling with and adjusting the network of wires coming from the machine. The horned sky whales circled closer and closer, dancing against a shimmering display of Emerald Fire.

'I just can't seem to switch off the signal,' frowned Lotti, her snout so close to the whirring mechanism that Zeina was worried she might catch her whiskers.

'I could cut the power,' a whispered voice came from the floor. Zeina was relieved Sparks was speaking in front of Lotti. It meant she really trusted her and somehow it renewed Zeina's faith in her also.

'Won't that just stop any more whales from coming this way? What about those that are already here?' Zeina asked, looking up at the shadows that had grown closer.

'I . . .' Lotti's voice trailed off as it dawned on her. 'I don't know. I had hoped we would have managed to cut the signal before they arrived. I guess we'll just have to hope that they'll turn round.'

Something heavy settled in Zeina's stomach. If only they could let the whales know—

'Wait, I have an idea!' Zeina said. 'Instead of switching off the signal, could we change the message so that it's a warning instead?'

'That's a great idea, Zeina!' said Lotti. 'It shouldn't be too tricky to reverse the signal.' She glanced up, the Smara Ignis reflecting jade and turquoise cascades in her eyes. A silvery-white shape flew directly over the thicket, casting them for a moment into darkness. 'I just wish we had a bit more time – they are so close now,' she breathed.

'Come on,' Zeina said firmly. 'You can do this.'

Lotti nodded, and after a few more moments of huffing and tinkering, the cogs and springs inside the machine seemed to judder and then stop. She breathed, her ears relaxing. 'That's better. Now, if I just—'

She reached back inside, prodding and prising with her tools. There was a clunk and then the mechanisms sprang back to life. They sounded different somehow – the cogs turning with a steady purr.

'That's it.' Lotti sat back and took in a deep breath. She smiled at Zeina and Sparks, pink tongue panting.

'What does the message say now?' asked Zeina, craning her ear towards the bell of the horn, despite the fact she knew she would never hear it.

'It doesn't say words exactly,' Lotti explained. 'It's more like a feeling. It's now a feeling of foreboding – it signals for them to get away from this place. Come on, let's get out of these trees to have a better look.'

The thicket of trees around the machine had shielded them from much of what was going on outside. As they crept towards the mountainside, the trees thinned. Peeking out from the edge of the rocky outcrop, Zeina gasped. Horned sky whales, hundreds of them, had gathered around the mountaintop. The sun, on the cusp of the horizon, lit their silvery undersides with a resplendent shine. They flew in little groups, the smaller ones darting and jostling to be at the front, the beat of their tails quickening as they raced. The largest ones sailed overhead, some with magnificent twisted tusks jutting out several metres in front of them. Many of the smallest whales had two shorter horns where their tusks should be, or no tusks at all.

'Don't all horned sky whales grow tusks?' Zeina whispered.

'It's mainly the males, and they don't develop fully until they're a year or two old,' Lotti explained.

'So that means only the male whales they caught could be

turned into Osiris Whales and sold?' Zeina whispered. 'What would Dr Mortwell do if he caught a female?'

'Well, I can't *imagine* he would just let it go,' Lotti replied.

Sparks shook her head and shuddered, her eyes alight with terror. 'He would use them for experiments,' she whispered close to Zeina's ear. 'Many whales never make it out of a STANS facility alive.'

Zeina grabbed Sparks's hand and gave it what she hoped was a reassuring squeeze – that was the most Sparks had ever spoken aloud to Zeina, and as far as she knew, the most she had shared with anyone about her life before the Smog Rats rescued her.

A loud whirring focused their attention on the valley below. Those metal teeth across the entrance to the underground STANS facility were creaking open.

'Does that mean that Jackson and Shrapnel have managed to free the whale?' Zeina asked excitedly, watching the opening for any glimpse of a whale tusk.

Lotti frowned. 'If so, we should soon see it. The king won't want it free inside the facility with them. That opening could equally just mean that Dr Mortwell is getting ready for the hunt. It doesn't look like any of the investors know we are here yet.'

Despite the billow of black smoke coming from the mine behind the mountain, it appeared that so far Mortwell, Steele

221

and Hamilton were continuing with their plan. The glass-fronted building was lit up by floodlights as a stream of Aboves made their way up a spiral staircase to emerge on a grand platform on top of the mountain. Zeina got out her spyglass to have a closer look. The ladies and gentlemen were all dressed up as if they were attending a party rather than a whale hunt. They sipped champagne as waiting staff brought round platters of canapés. Some chatted excitedly in little groups and others stared at the awesome spectacle that surrounded them through their own spyglasses or binoculars.

A particularly large whale flew right past their outcrop, swooping up towards a group of about five young whales. Up close, Zeina could make out the dark corkscrew patterns within the horn. Its white belly was mottled silver and grey in a pattern that reminded her of ice cracking across a frozen lake. Its flippers were much shorter than the sky whales she had seen before and its tail flukes more rounded. Their lumina lines were less obvious than those of a wild sky whale, streaks of silver along their backs that glistened rather than glowed.

'It's working,' Lotti whispered. 'The older ones are starting to herd up the younger ones from their pod. There are at least five different pods here – horned sky whales might be shy of humans, but they are pretty sociable with each other. The young ones are very excited; they've probably never been around so many of their own kind. It'll take the adults a while to get them away from here.'

'Still, they won't fly into the trap, not now we've changed the message, surely?' Zeina asked.

'No.' Lotti paused, looking nervously down at the harpoons further down the mountainside. 'But once Dr Mortwell works out their transmitter in no longer working, he could always instruct the guards to use the harpoons to scare them into the valley. It's not quite what Steele promised the investors, but better that than no whales at all.'

An almighty bang rang out across the valley, and there was a sudden surge in the smoke coming from the mine. Exclamations echoed from the investors, excited chatter giving way to shock. The floodlights blinked off and on, and then bit by bit the whole of the building was cast into darkness. Zeina heard screams and shouts coming from the viewing platform. An alarm blared.

'That'll be Katu,' Sparks whispered.

'Maybe,' Lotti said. 'But if the power is off down there . . .' She closed her eyes again and listened. 'The power cut has switched off our warning too – the whales are confused. If the investors start to panic now and try to leave in their airships, any whale that is still in the area will be fired at by dart guns and harpoons . . . It'll be a bloodbath.'

'Oh no!' Zeina gasped.

The sound of pistols reverberated from somewhere below, making Zeina wince. She hoped her friends were all safe.

'The *Nightjar* could arrive any time. We need to get the power back to that machine,' Zeina said, imagining her dad and Captain Parr desperately trying to dodge hundreds of scared, angry horned sky whales and a whole fleet of harpoon-equipped airships.

Lotti looked across the valley, where the morning sun was just breaching the horizon, bleeding a fiery orange into the sky. She removed her backpack and took from inside it a little glass dome with a tangle of wires coming from it.

'My solar tech!' Zeina exclaimed in surprise, quite forgetting where she was and who she was talking to. '*You* stole it?'

'I *borrowed* it – for safekeeping,' Lotti explained. 'When Katu and I set off, I knew it would only be a matter of time before the king's guards realised something was up. I was worried that when they found out I was missing they might search my workshop. I didn't want your technology getting damaged or taken.'

There was more pistol fire, screams from the viewing platform and then a deadly clanging of metal. Zeina caught sight of one of the harpoon guns as it began to creak into life.

Lotti handed Zeina her prototype. 'Do you think you and Sparks could use this to power up the echophone machine?

The sun is nearly up – we haven't got much time. We need that machine up and running to warn the whales to get away, before any of them get hurt.'

Sparks examined the wires sceptically and shrugged.

'This little prototype will never be strong enough to power that machine on its own!' Zeina cried.

'It's a good job I made a few more then,' Lotti purred, handing Zeina her backpack, where inside there were at least ten replicas of her prototype. Zeina didn't know whether to be angry or relieved.

'But where will you be?' Sparks asked, her voice tiny but clear.

Lotti's claws raked the frozen ground. 'I need to make sure no one operates those harpoons,' she snarled.

CHAPTER 24

The loss of power plunged the underground facility into darkness. It took Jackson a moment or two for his eyes to become accustomed to the dark, but the king wasted no time at all. Awoken from his slump, he hurled his full weight at the hatch door. Jackson crouched, arms over his head, as great chunks of rock and clouds of dust rained from the ceiling of the cave. There was the clash of claws on metal and then an almighty clang as the net crashed to the floor. They were free – from the net at least.

Jackson peeked from under his arms, watching the large shape of the king pounce towards the figure of Dr Mortwell, knocking him to floor. Claws ripped, teeth gnashed and the device that controlled the whale went skidding across the floor.

Jackson snapped out of his trance – this was his chance to free the whale! He had to disconnect the last bit of the STAN system while he still could. Frantically, he searched the floor of the cave until his hand traced across a metal tool, a criss-cross of blades, hinged at the middle. Pliers! Just what he needed. Now that the device which controlled the whale lay abandoned on the cave floor, the whale itself seemed to have been put back on pause. It hovered in the air at just above Jackson's head height. The white of its hide seemed almost to glow from the darkness of the cave recess. Jackson tried to block out the roars of the king, a high-pitched scream from Dr Mortwell and a whimpering from Hamilton somewhere nearby. His hands reached up to the hide, feeling as gently as he could up the ridged skin and underneath the last remaining part of the harness. The whale bucked in pain, its tusks making a dreadful scraping against the cave wall.

'Nearly there,' soothed Jackson. 'Nearly there.'

Soon his hand found the bundle of wires again. Jackson gripped them, keeping his fist tight while he gently edged the pliers to where he needed them using his other hand. It took all his strength to cut through the wires one by one. *Snap. Snap. Snap.* The whale jolted and tossed a little more with every wire severed. It lifted Jackson's feet clear from the floor, but Jackson held on, swinging from his pliers. The final snap, and Jackson fell to the floor with a heavy thud. The whale was free! It thrashed its tail, causing the last part of the STAN system and harness to fall from its back. Jackson rolled, his hands and forearms raised to cover his face as the glass dome smashed. He flinched, fragments of glass hailing down around him.

He opened his eyes. The whale had flown up and then rounded on Jackson, two giant tusks coming straight for where he lay. The upper part of the harness had left deep cuts in the whale's hide.

'No,' he yelled, holding out his palms. 'Please don't!'

The whale snorted, an angry roar that reverberated around the cave.

Distracted from his fury, the king rose up on his hind legs. A dark red stained the fur of his chest. Mortwell made no attempt to move.

A terrified squeal from Hamilton drew the whale towards where he cowered.

'No!' he cried, backing as far into a corner as he possibly could. 'I—Not me—It wasn't me—Please, no!'

From the inside pocket of his tailcoat Hamilton retrieved a tiny silver pistol and held it in front of him. It shook uncontrollably in his hands. Eyes closed, he fired wildly into the air. BANG. BANG. BANG.

The first bullet hit one of the machines, which began to crackle and smoke. The second zipped towards the Emerald King, who roared in anger. The third narrowly missed Jackson, leaving a smoking dent in the cavern wall just above his head. But none of them stopped the whale. The pistol fire seemed only to have enraged the beast further. It homed in on Hamilton, tusks thrashing wildly.

Jackson covered his face. Despite all that his uncle had done, he couldn't bear to watch the whale pierce him with those tusks. He waited for the screams, yet they didn't come.

Instead, the door of the facility was flung open and Shrapnel and Katu burst through. Shrapnel rushed towards the king, who had slumped forward on top of Dr Mortwell. They both lay very still. Katu flinched as he stood up on his hind legs. He raised his paws high into the air. His eyes were closed, ears cocked, and Jackson knew he was trying to communicate with the whale.

'Go!' he shouted out loud. 'Leave now, while you can.'

And the whale swooped around in a wide arc, its tusks scraping through the wall of machines and cutting them to pieces. It rounded on Katu, and Jackson was sure it would slice him in two as easily as it had the machines. Katu stood calm and commanding, as the beast roared and thrashed towards him.

'No!' Jackson begged. He got to his feet, unsure what he could do but desperate to do *something*. The whale was so close; a second later and it would collide with Katu. Jackson lunged uselessly, knocking Katu to the floor just as the whale beat its tail, changing direction to swoop up into the chute and out of the hole in the cave's ceiling.

From the cavern floor Jackson watched the whale, free from its harness, fly up through the open shutters and into the freedom of the awakening dawn.

CHAPTER 25

Zeina and Sparks crouched at the base of the echophone machine, their heads bowed together, working as quickly as they could. Zeina readied each solar device, unscrewing the lens, pipetting more drops of purple lilaberry juice underneath and then securing it back in place. She tested each device using a lightbulb, before handing it to Sparks. The last thing they wanted was an explosion; that would alert the lawkeepers to their presence.

Sparks busied herself with a pair of pliers. The tangle of different-coloured wires made no sense to Zeina at all, and yet Sparks seemed to be able to read them like a map.

'It's disconnected from the mains,' she whispered. 'Now . . . just need to wire . . . in each device.'

Zeina tried to focus on testing the ones that were left – she was about halfway through, but knew they would need every single one working if they were to have any chance of powering the machine and warning the whales. It was fiddly and time-consuming – time they didn't really have. It occurred to Zeina that in future it would work better if they were all attached together in a strip or panel. If only she had worked harder on the solar tech when she had the chance! Numb and shivering, her fingers fumbled and she dropped the little screwdriver she was holding, which rolled away.

'Damn!' she exclaimed, rooting around in the snow to find it again.

Sparks handed it to her.

'You can do this, Zeina,' she said, her large eyes staring intently, her white-blonde spikes dancing in the new sunlight.

And somehow the words felt powerful, hearing them aloud from Sparks's own mouth.

They worked on, the rising sun lighting up the clearing a little more with each passing minute. Soon golden beams sneaked through the maze of branches, illuminating the ground in gleaming stripes. Sparks positioned each lens in a place with maximum sunlight; the network of wires connecting them to the machine made a web across the white ground. The machine fluttered to life, cogs turning and spluttering, before clunking to a stop.

'We just need a couple more,' Sparks murmured.

'We only have one!' Zeina called back, tightening the last screw and connecting it to a little lightbulb to test.

Their heads jerked suddenly from their task. There was the sound of more pistol fire but close by this time, just the other side of the thicket. Zeina's heart leapt into her throat. What if that had been aimed at Lotti? Was she lying somewhere, injured?

'Here.' Zeina handed the last lens to Sparks. 'I'll sneak through to see what's going on. That's the last one, Sparks. I hope it's enough.'

Zeina crept low to the ground in the direction of the pistol fire. Whales circled overhead, casting strange moving shadows across the rocky undergrowth. Spotting movement a little way in front of her, Zeina ducked down further. Through the branches she could just make out someone's head, covered in a green hat. It wasn't a cap like the lawkeepers wore, it was woolly and covered in a fine gold pattern.

'Nedra?' she called, before she could stop herself.

The hat wheeled around, revealing Nedra's grey eyes, wide with concern.

'Zeina?' she whispered. Zeina stood up slowly and Nedra ran over to her, scooping her up in an enormous hug. Zeina's body flooded with relief that her friend was here and she was OK. Plus, Nedra was a spy, a fully fledged member of the Smog Rats. They could use her help.

'Oh, Zeina, I'm so glad you're all right. I've been so worried.'

'*You've* been worried? Where were you? How did you even—'

'There's no time to explain now. Come on!' Nedra grabbed Zeina's hand, hurrying her out from the thicket and down a narrow mountain path.

'Nedra, wait—' Zeina could hear the same distant whirring of machinery, cogs that stuttered and then stopped. Sparks might need her help. She tried to pull away but Nedra's grip only tightened.

'There's no time, Zeina. It's your dad, he's hurt!'

Panic surged inside Zeina. Her dad was here already? The *Nightjar* must be in trouble – it could have been damaged by a horned sky whale or even a harpoon. Zeina gripped Nedra's hand tightly and together they ran down the winding rocky path.

A squawk from above alerted Zeina to the presence of Albi. His great wingspan circled overhead but he seemed agitated, his croaks higher in tone and more urgent than usual. He swooped down, his claws narrowly missing the top of Zeina's head.

'It's all right, Albi,' Zeina panted, waving him away. 'I'm coming as fast as I can.' He circled again, cawing angrily in an upward spiral, before transforming into a flash and disappearing.

Rounding a tight cliff-edge corner, Zeina was stopped in

her tracks by the sight of an airship. However, this airship was most certainly *not* the *Nightjar*. Sleek and painted in silver and black stripes that stretched nose to tail, it had no wings or smog chamber but pistons and funnels that bellowed great clouds of black smoke. The smell of burning ore, at one time so familiar to Zeina, now made her choke. To the front of the airship, two enormous harpoon guns glinted in the sunlight.

The airship's name, painted in silver letters, caught her eye.

RAVEN II

Time seemed to slow as the familiar figure climbed down the narrow gangway. Vivianne Steele had changed out of her evening wear into a green flight suit with a white fur collar. Her chestnut curls were held from her face by a golden pair of aviator goggles that rested on her forehead.

'Surprise! Isn't she glorious, Zeina?' her voice sang, so light and happy it sent shivers down Zeina's spine.

Hoping that Nedra had had the sense to run, Zeina wheeled around. But as she turned, she found that Nedra was in fact standing calmly behind her, smiling and blocking her escape.

'Nedra, what are you doing?'

'I'm finally getting my revenge.' Her smoky eyes danced with satisfaction. She advanced on Zeina, pushing her closer and closer to Steele and the gangway.

'Revenge for what? What are you talking about?'

Was Nedra joking? Was this some kind of ploy to distract Steele so they could escape? She searched Nedra's face for a telltale wink or the hint of a smirk, but she seemed deadly serious.

'Revenge for my mother.' Nedra's lips curled into a savage grimace.

'Wh—What?'

'Oh, didn't you know?' Steele said. 'Nedra's surname is Wilson. Her dear mother was part of my crew on the *Raven*.'

'I bet you don't even *remember* her,' Nedra hissed, tears spilling down pink cheeks.

'I do remember her,' Zeina said quietly.

In fact, Zeina remembered Wilson rather well – a tall, fierce woman. She remembered being restrained by her on Steele's orders. She remembered Wilson jeering at her, carrying her like a log to her cabin, roughly throwing her inside and then bolting the door. Other than Zeina giving Wilson a few swift kicks in the struggle against her captor, she could not imagine what Nedra was seeking revenge for.

'But I still don't understand,' Zeina admitted.

'She *died* because of you,' Nedra spat. 'In the airship crash *you* caused over Howlingwood. She was working to pay for my release from the mining grounds. She nearly had enough money saved. And then one day she never came back.'

'When I escaped from the wreckage,' Steele purred, 'I needed help to stay hidden. I remembered Nedra was in the mining grounds and felt I owed it to her to let her know how the last person she had in the world had died. Exactly *who* was to blame. And Nedra has been so helpful in setting all this up; she really is quite the talent.'

From a little bag Nedra retrieved a pair of round spectacles and put them on. The sight of her made Zeina's stomach somersault and yet she couldn't quite put her finger on what was wrong. Nedra replaced her woollen hat with a neat black wig, but it wasn't until she pressed the little black beard to her chin that Zeina realised.

'The man from the presentation, the one who visited the Emerald King and made the deal for land in return for the lost emeralds,' she gasped. 'It was you?'

Vivianne chuckled as Nedra changed her expression, magically becoming the bearded man.

'A true master of disguise! I remembered that both Nedra and her mother were part of a gang of con-artists and pickpockets before they were arrested and sent to the mining grounds. After I escaped, I went to retrieve the Palik treasure I had hidden in my secret vault. I knew that I would need help in making the deal in secret and Nedra really has been perfect. Now you're the last piece of the puzzle, Zeina.' Steele laughed. 'The final part we need before we start our adventure

237

together. This adventure is the one I've been waiting for my *entire* life.'

'I'm not going anywhere with either of you,' Zeina said firmly.

'Come now, Zeina,' Steele cooed. 'I don't want to hurt your friends, but I will if I have to.' She pointed at the harpoon guns. Zeina thought about Jackson and Shrapnel and Katu all down there somewhere in Steele's facility. She thought about Lotti and Sparks, so exposed on the mountainside. They all just needed a little more time. It was sunrise – the *Nightjar* would be here soon. She had to stall Steele somehow.

Nedra, who had replaced her disguise inside her bag, grabbed Zeina by the shoulder and roughly shoved her towards the gangway. Zeina weighed up her limited options. The narrow path back up to Sparks was blocked by Nedra, and the *Raven II* was blocking her only way down the mountain. She could try to push past, make a run for it but, realistically, how far would she get? And who might get hurt when Steele came after her?

Deciding it would be much safer for her friends, Zeina allowed herself to be frogmarched up the gangway and on to the deck of Steele's airship.

CHAPTER 26

'No, no, no,' Hamilton whimpered from the corner of the cave. He rocked backwards and forwards in the murky gloom, wringing his hands. Alarms blared from behind the STANS facility door but inside it all felt strangely quiet.

'We must move quickly,' Katu groaned, heaving himself back up on to all fours. One back leg hung uselessly.

'I'm sorry, Katu. I was trying—I thought—' Jackson spluttered.

Katu bowed his head, his gold eyes gleaming with gratitude.

'You thought the whale would attack me,' he smiled. 'You tried to save my life, Jackson. There's nothing to be sorry about.'

A lamp spluttered to life, the complete destruction of the facility becoming clear. Crates had been knocked on to their sides, shards from the smashed-up STAN system scattered the floor and every one of the machines was broken and smoking.

'Oh! It's all ruined! What will I tell the investors?' Hamilton babbled desperately. He looked around him, his face ghostly pale. His golden monocle lay smashed beside him and the silver pistol, now quite forgotten, at his feet.

Katu limped over, snatched it from the floor and stowed it in the pocket of his travelling cloak. Shrapnel had his lantern held up high to better see the motionless Emerald King. He reached down into the fur around his neck and felt around for a pulse.

'He's alive,' Shrapnel whispered. 'But only just. Jackson, give me a hand.'

Jackson gulped, trying to imagine that the red stickiness that stained the king's snowy fur was something other than blood. Katu limped across and together they managed to haul the king off Dr Mortwell. Jackson swayed when he caught a glimpse of the scientist's injuries. He turned his back – he didn't need to see any more.

'Oh!' Hamilton cried. 'Oh, Mortwell. Is he . . . ? Is he . . . ?— Oh! But what do I—'

They all ignored Hamilton's babbling and focused on the king. His eyes were tightly closed, but now he was on his back Jackson could see the gentle rise and fall of his chest. Katu checked his pulse and nodded.

'You're correct, Shrapnel. He's alive, but we must move fast. There's no telling how much of this blood is his and how much is Mortwell's. One of Hamilton's bullets hit him. Look here.' He pointed to a red patch on the king's abdomen. 'And the whale's tusks have wounded him here.' He examined a deep slice through the king's shoulder. 'He won't be able to walk out of here, and he needs help *urgently*.'

'What's happening?' Jackson whispered. 'Outside that door, what's going on?'

'They're evacuating the area,' Katu explained calmly. 'The fire in the mine was a good distraction but it was only a matter of time before they put it out. I managed to set off the alarms across the facility. Then, when I was on my way to see if you needed help, I bumped into Shrapnel.'

'I'd heard footsteps coming as soon as I left the facility and managed to hide just in time,' Shrapnel explained. 'When I saw Mortwell go inside, I knew you'd be caught. I knew we'd need a plan to get you out and it was lucky I found Katu when I did. We decided the only way was to cut the power to the whole facility.'

'It caused complete panic. The investors won't stick around for long,' Katu nodded. 'And the lawkeepers will follow.'

'What about Steele?' Jackson asked.

'I haven't seen a trace of her since that presentation,' Katu replied. 'And from my eavesdropping, nobody else has either. She and her intermediary, the man with the black beard, have completely disappeared with much of the money.'

'They've taken my *money*,' Hamilton cried. 'It's *gone*. And the facility. My shares—It'll all be worthless now—' He was swaying violently, gabbling to no one in particular.

'How are we going to get the king out?' Jackson asked. 'He's far too heavy to carry and there'll be lawkeepers everywhere.'

Katu thought for a moment, his eyes resting on one of the only cages that remained upright on its wheels. It was lined up next to the net – ready for the whale hunt as if nothing had happened.

'We'll have to use that to carry him. There's an exit on to the ice plain just down the corridor. It was guarded, but hopefully they will have left by now.'

'We can't just waltz out of the door with the King of the Feln in a whale cage!' Shrapnel shook his head. 'No matter how much of a hullabaloo is going on, we only need *one* lawkeeper to spot us and we're done for!'

'No, we'll need a disguise.' Katu looked around the facility for inspiration.

'Where's Ned's bag when you need it!' Shrapnel joked.

Jackson was the one who spotted it first – the black, high-collared lab coat hanging in the corner of the cave. A spare that Mortwell was unlikely to ever need again.

Jackson put it on. It was stiff and itchy and much too big. No one would mistake him for Dr Mortwell, but with a pair of goggles on he would pass for a scientist of some kind.

'What about Shrapnel?' he asked.

'I have an idea for that,' Katu replied, walking over to Hamilton, now thankfully silent but still pale with shock, and rocking, his knees curled up to his chest.

Hamilton had always been a coward. Happy to enjoy the luxuries of life but not wanting to lift a finger to do anything to get them himself. Whether it was killing Jackson's parents or getting rid of Jackson, he'd always arranged for the dirty work to be outsourced. He shied away from anything remotely unpleasant. The trauma and bloodshed he had just witnessed had obviously been far too much for his sensitive nerves.

'Give me your tailcoat and hat, please, Hamilton,' Katu said quietly.

'My hat? My beautiful tailcoat? Why?' His eyes were so panic-stricken that Jackson almost felt sorry for him.

'Hand them over, please,' Katu asked again without raising his voice. 'I would hate to have to use this, but I will if you force me.' He took Hamilton's silver pistol from his pocket and pointed it at him.

'Oh! No. But the hat is . . . one of my favourites. Are you quite sure you need it?'

'I'm afraid so,' replied Katu, shaking the pistol slightly.

Hamilton's hands shuddered as he removed his hat and tailcoat and gave them to Katu, who passed them on to Shrapnel.

Jackson looked at Shrapnel and frowned. He could see that, even with Hamilton's luxurious coat and hat, Shrapnel made a most unlikely Above investor. His trousers and snow boots, much like Jackson's, were scuffed and muddy, and Shrapnel still had the big swollen wound across his cheek, from where the chandelier had sliced into him.

'It's the best we can do for now. With all the chaos going on around you, you should pass from a distance.' Katu sighed. 'My leg means I won't be much use to you from a pushing point of view. But I should be able to keep to the shadows up ahead and warn you of any danger.'

'How do we get him in the cage?' Jackson asked, eyeing up the enormous king, still slumped on the cave floor.

Katu took off his travelling cloak. Together they were able to roll the king on to it and use it like a sling to heave his great body up into the cage. Then they covered him over with the cloak, tucking it around his fur, so that no one could see what they were transporting. Jackson prayed that no one would look too closely. It seemed almost impossible that they would all get out without being discovered, and yet it was their only hope.

Together he and Shrapnel had just about enough strength to push the cage forward on its wheels.

'Oh—Don't go—' Hamilton blubbed when he saw them push the cage towards the door. 'Please—Don't leave me here alone—' He stared very hard at Jackson as if he had forgotten completely who he was. 'Jackson? Come now—Me and Herbert are all you have left . . . Especially after my dear brother—'

The anger that Jackson had been pushing down in all the months that had passed since he had seen Hamilton last bubbled over and then erupted. He lost all control, turning towards his uncle in a thunderous rage.

'Jackson, ignore him.' Katu's voice drifted, muffled by the red mist that flooded Jackson's brain.

'He *has* to be punished for what he's done,' Jackson boomed. 'He has to be stopped, or else he'll just find a way to ruin everything, like he always does.'

Jackson caught sight of something glistening on the floor of the cave near one of the broken machines – the pistol; Hamilton's pistol. It must have skidded from Katu's pocket when they draped his cloak over the king. It looked so small, like a toy, and yet Jackson had seen the damage it had done.

Jackson dashed towards it, but this sudden movement seemed to startle Hamilton into action. Before Jackson could reach it, Hamilton had leapt up, grabbing desperately around Jackson's neck. Jackson could hear Shrapnel's and Katu's shouts and yet not make out a word they were saying.

Hamilton had him now by the lapels of the lab coat. He raised him off the ground with a strength that surprised Jackson. Hamilton's wild eyes bored into his.

'You are *still* a Willoughby, Jackson,' Hamilton ranted. 'Willoughbys must do everything we need to stay on top. These Belows will *never* understand – they *belong* beneath us. They cannot be in charge. I was only doing my—'

'Let him go,' Shrapnel's voice broke through, cold and clear. In his hand, the silver pistol gleamed.

Hamilton drew back, dropping Jackson like a stone.

'Come, Jackson.' Katu beckoned. 'Come on, leave him. He has nothing left. His money is gone, the facility destroyed – he is desperate.'

Jackson scrambled away, but Shrapnel did not lower the pistol.

'Jackson's right,' he spat, giving Hamilton a vengeful stare. He was back to cowering on the cave floor. Head bowed and arms raised in surrender, he let out an unintelligible whimper. 'He hasn't been punished,' Shrapnel continued. 'He still has Willoughby Towers, jewels, gold, Above friends who will help him.'

'There's *nothing* we can do now, Shrapnel,' Katu said sternly. 'We need to concentrate on getting out *safely*. We must leave him here. Let him go.'

'It should be up to Jackson,' Shrapnel growled. 'We can arrest him. Hold him prisoner on the *Nightjar*. Or maybe I should just shoot him.'

Hamilton shrieked, begging. Jackson wasn't sure whether Shrapnel really would pull the trigger or whether he was just enjoying the fear and panic on Hamilton's face.

'Jackson, we must leave now,' Katu implored. 'Hamilton will only slow us down. We have to get out and check that Zeina and the others are OK. They might need our help.'

Jackson watched as his uncle pleaded, scrabbling on his knees on the floor of the cave. Without his fine clothes or powerful friends he was quite the pathetic figure and Jackson felt a little of his all-consuming rage begin to ebb away. But in the end it was the image of Zeina trapped somewhere, needing help, that made up Jackson's mind once and for all.

'Leave him,' he said firmly to Shrapnel.

And with one last, long, pitying look at Hamilton, he turned towards the door.

CHAPTER 27

I t felt so strange to Zeina to be watching Steele once again at the helm of an airship. The *Raven II* was nowhere near as large as the original *Raven*, Steele's legendary airship that Zeina had travelled on last year, and yet there were so many details that were *just* the same. Steele's desk, littered with maps, was just as untidy as the one Zeina and Steele had used to plan the route from the Willoughby Whale to Howlingwood. There were the same floor-to-ceiling windows, a velvet high-backed chair for Steele to captain from and even a little table where her famous golden spyglass rested. Like Steele, the spyglass seemed to have escaped the wreckage of the first *Raven* with minimal damage.

The *Raven II*'s smaller size meant the engine room was attached to the cockpit itself. One side was left completely open to the deck to allow any extra heat from the furnace to escape. Nedra shovelled ore into the flames and then swung shut the iron door. Steele turned winches and pressed buttons. The steady clank of the pistons began to speed up.

Despite the amount of time that had passed since she'd travelled on one, the sounds of an ore-powered airship were imprinted on Zeina's brain from all those years growing up on an airship platform. She could sense that it would only be a matter of minutes before it had enough power to take off. She had to stall – keep them busy for a little longer and then try to escape or hope that someone would work out where she was and come to rescue her.

'A smaller airship is much more economical,' Steele grinned. 'And now I'm out of the whaling game, really there was no need for such an enormous airship or a large crew. I can pilot this one completely alone if I need to, although an extra pair of hands is always useful.'

'Out of the whaling game?' Zeina spluttered. 'You've just started a company that sells them!'

'Ah, yes, you saw my presentation!' Steele smiled. 'A lovely surprise! Nedra and I originally planned to come and lure you away from the Glacial Palace during the Equinox celebrations. But really it's so much easier this way! There's so much less to explain!'

'You *knew* where I was?' Zeina asked, confused. 'How?'

Nedra pointed to the whale brooch she had given to Zeina. It was still there shining on the collar of her thick winter coat.

'It's a bug,' Nedra explained. 'They are used a lot by spies who are tracking someone – a little transmitter sends a radio signal to a receiver.' She took out the little red whale brooch from her pocket – it was flashing quickly and brightly. 'I know exactly how far away you are from me at all times and can use it to follow you too. I knew you had set off from the Glacial Palace, I knew you had seen the facility, I knew you were in the room watching the presentation. Later, I knew you were near that machine and fired my pistol to draw you out. I knew you wouldn't be able to resist being at the centre of the action. And I was right – *you* came right to me!'

Zeina felt disgusted – the gift she had been so fond of had been a trap all along. She ripped it from her collar and threw it to the floor.

'That's a shame,' Nedra laughed, snatching it from the floor and pocketing it. 'I thought it really suited you.'

'But if you knew we were here, why didn't you try to stop us?' Zeina asked.

'Stop you and your friends destroying the facility, you mean?' Steele smirked. 'Stop you from sabotaging the transmitter? The truth is, Zeina, I'm done with all that. I've got what I came for.' She pointed to five large sacks, all packed with bank notes. 'I've taken the money the investors handed over tonight and sold all my shares in Osiris. I'm done with it all. I've had enough of Aboves – their greed, their snobbery. For all their idolisation of me as I built their fortunes for them, none of them cared when I "died".

She pulled down a lever with force, her voice full of spite. 'In the blink of an eye they were fighting over my jewels, my ore mines, selling them off to the highest bidder. There's no loyalty with them. It was people like Nedra here, people I knew in the mining grounds, those were the ones that I could trust to help me. No, I'm quite satisfied that you and your friends have ruined Hamilton's investments. I have stolen a fortune from Above families tonight. So, you see, now I'm an outlaw just like you!'

'You and I are *nothing* alike,' Zeina spat.

Steele frowned. 'We are both Belows and, just like Nedra here, we have had to fight for everything we have,' Steele replied. 'We're both fierce explorers. And we both do whatever it takes.'

The propellers began to whirr and the *Raven II* lifted ever so slightly from its mooring. Zeina couldn't get distracted by Steele's speeches; she had to stop the ship from taking off. Once in the air it would be impossible for her to escape. Nedra shovelled another load of ore into the furnace, the feverish heat making her cheeks glow scarlet.

'So what happens now?' Zeina asked, desperately wracking her brain for ideas.

'My plans are unchanged from last year. As is my offer to you, Zeina. With this ship and all this lovely money, I have the means to do as I please. Free from the whims of those selfish Above families, I will explore the parts of our continents that no human has explored before. We will travel north. I have enough supplies aboard to last us many months.'

'But why take *me*?' Zeina asked. 'The Smog Rats will come looking for me.'

'Ah, but they won't attack the airship – not while you are aboard. In fact, if I were to threaten your life, I'm quite certain they'd leave us well alone.' Her eyes gleamed and Zeina couldn't remember what she ever saw in this woman. 'You are to be a sort of . . . *hostage*, I guess. Although I do hope that, in time, you will begin to enjoy our adventures together once more.' She reached out to brush one of Zeina's stray curls behind her ear, an action that at one time would have made Zeina's heart swell. Zeina wanted to push her away, and yet the more time she spent talking to Zeina, the less time Steele was spending flying the airship. It hovered about a metre from the mountainside now. Nedra left the cockpit and began to untie the rope that moored the *Raven II* to a treetop.

The sun had risen clear of the horizon and the sky was full of airships flying south, the Above investors disappearing as quickly as they could from the sudden unexpected chaos of the facility. Zeina noticed that the horned sky whales were beginning to disperse too, their shadows against the new sun growing smaller. Sparks had done it! She just had to hope that Jackson, Shrapnel and the king had managed to free the prototype whale and got themselves somewhere safe. Now released from its mooring, Zeina knew the airship would drift until Steele piloted it – she just had to keep her talking a little longer.

'You are so loyal, Zeina.' Steele's eyes burned with an emerald fire. 'A quality of yours that I have always admired. And yet you long for adventure, just as I do! It can't be easy for you, following Captain Parr's instructions all the time – tinkering with your inventions, while your friends and family risk their lives. Nedra tells me you are left *quite* out of the action – stuck inside much of the time doing repairs. For that you might as well have stayed in Ravenport.'

'You tried to kill me,' Zeina gasped. 'You were going to leave me in the mining grounds. Why do you want me to join you now?'

'Well, you see, Zeina. After the crash, I developed a new perspective on things. And while Nedra is a marvellous spy,' Steele whispered, 'you are a truly talented innovator, Zeina. An engineer, an adventurer – just like me. Two peas in a pod. You have principles and you stick to them. A leader, not a follower.'

She began to turn a winch ever so slightly; the *Raven II* began to turn north.

'And now that the veil of fame and fortune has been lifted from my eyes, I have learned to appreciate loyalty, courage and ingenuity above all else,' Steele continued, turning back to Zeina, staring at her intently. 'I can think of no one better than *you* to be my second. And I always get what I want in the end. We became so close last year – truly, I began to think of you as a daughter. I was far too harsh on you when you decided that you couldn't betray Jackson. I know that, once we have discovered new places together, we can rekindle that closeness we once had.'

Zeina's heart thudded. There was no way she would join Steele willingly, forget about the Smog Rats, her friends and her dad. And yet when Steele had said the words 'as a daughter', pain knifed through her chest, for if she was honest with herself there were times last year where she had begun to think of Steele like a mother.

'You said we would kill her.' Nedra's voice, flinty and cold, came from the open side of the cockpit – she had returned from untying the mooring. 'You said *I* was to be your second. That *I* was like a daughter to you.'

'Now, Nedra,' Steele said evenly, as if she were talking to an unreasonable child.

'You said I would have revenge for my mother's death,' Nedra bellowed. 'You *promised*.'

Despite Nedra's betrayal, Zeina felt sorry for the girl. She knew what it felt like to discover you'd been lied to by someone you admired. The muscles on Vivianne's neck stiffened as she wound in the winch. The airship rose, turning with some speed. 'There's no reason to kill Zeina, not if she decides to join us,' Steele said, scowling, her lips pinched. Zeina's heart hammered – she didn't know whether Steele had been lying to Nedra or was lying to her now, but she didn't care. All she knew was that she had to find a way off the airship fast!

'Liar!' Nedra yelled as she launched herself at Steele, knocking her away from the airship's controls.

Nedra and Steele fought on the floor of the *Raven II*. Steele tried desperately to grab on to the controls and haul herself up but Nedra was stronger than she looked. They struggled, rolling towards the open side of the cockpit.

Zeina wasted no time, running for the controls and directing the airship back towards the mountain. She turned and saw that Steele had managed to right herself. The vicious explorer elbowed Nedra back to the floor. Nedra banged her head on the railings and lay stunned upon the deck. In horror, Zeina watched as Steele began to push and shove Nedra under the bottom railing. Before she knew what was happening, Nedra's feet, legs and belly were hanging off the deck of the airship like a rag doll. She came to, eyes wide with panic, scrambling with her hands against the wood.

'No, stop!' Zeina called, abandoning the controls and rushing over to where Steele was now prising Nedra's hand from the surface of the deck. The rest of Nedra swung in the air. She screamed – the mountain closer than before, yet still many metres below her.

'Don't!' Zeina yelled at Steele, trying to grab on to Nedra's wrist. 'You'll kill her!'

Steele pushed Zeina away.

'She is no use to me now anyway.' Steele's cruel lips twisted. Nedra cried out, desperately trying to find something to grab on to with her other hand – but there was nothing.

What occurred next seemed to happen in slow motion. Zeina tried to get there in time but it was as if her whole body had slowed down. One by one, Steele levered Nedra's fingers from their hold. Nedra screamed as she fell, landing with an ugly thud on the very edge of an outcrop. Her body, limp and motionless, was stopped from falling down the mountainside only by the roots of a few trees clinging to the rocks.

Steele laughed and returned to the controls. 'It's better like this,' she said coldly. 'She would have only got in our way.'

Zeina stood on the edge of the deck, looking down sadly at where Nedra lay. The *Raven II* turned again, lurching around in an arc to fly north. For a moment the facility on the other side of the mountain came into view. The glass front glinted in the brilliant sunlight. Last night's storm had cleared the skies and Zeina closed her eyes for a second, basking in their bright blueness. The horned sky whales, tiny black spots now, looked like birds. She wondered if there would still be a feast today at the Glacial Palace for the Equinox.

She scoured the skies. There were no Above airships left now but no sight of the *Nightjar* either. No one would get there in time to rescue her – she would have to rescue herself.

Something far below Zeina caught her eye and a plan began to form; it was extremely dangerous, even for her, and yet it was her only chance. Would it be better to just stay where she was? She climbed over the railings, daring to peek down at the landscape as it rushed by beneath her.

'What are you doing?' Vivianne yelled from her controls. 'Jump? Don't be ridiculous, Zeina, we're far too high!'

Zeina took two deep breaths and let go with one arm, leaning over into the wind to face the craggy snow-covered mountaintops. Just a few seconds longer.

'Zeina!' Steele cried, and when she turned Zeina was surprised by the concern in Steele's eyes. Vivianne let go of the winch and ran to the railings.

But it was too late.

Zeina counted. ONE. TWO. THREE.

And jumped off the deck of Steele's airship.

CHAPTER 28

The brilliance of the new sun made Jackson flinch as they pushed the cage containing the king out of the exit from the cave system. To Jackson, it felt as though he had been in darkness for a long time. He blinked, watching the bright beams scatter across the great expanse. The gleaming snow of the mountains was almost blinding. A trail of dark-grey smoke still billowed from the mine, but the fire was now out and the machinery still and silent. An alarm blared distantly.

They had made slow progress inside the cave, pushing the king a little way before waiting for Katu to return to tell them the next part of the route was clear. At last they gave one great heave and the cage rolled out on to the ice plain. Shrapnel collapsed to the floor, leaning back against the cage and panting. Jackson, his limbs tingling, sagged down next to him. They had exited on to the glacier that flowed down the valley between this mountain and the next. Tracking up the valley, the giant whaling net gaped open and empty. Beyond that, three shining harpoon guns glinted at Jackson from the mountainside. His heart flipped. Thankfully they were abandoned – it seemed Aboves and lawkeepers alike had rushed to their airships in the panic. Distant black shadows buzzed like clouds of tiny insects across the sky. Jackson squinted into the brightness, yet he could not tell whether they were horned sky whales or airships, or both. Katu closed his eyes and listened.

'The others didn't turn off the signal,' Katu said. Jackson's heart sank. 'They did even better. They seem to have . . . reversed it.' Katu nodded, relieved. 'It has warned the sky whales it isn't safe here.'

Jackson, still too tired to speak, sighed in relief. Hopefully if they had managed to find the machine and reverse the signal, it meant that Lotti, Sparks and Zeina were all hiding somewhere together and safe.

From their position, the curve of the mountain obscured them from the front of the building but Jackson could see that the ice plain where the Above airships had been moored was now deserted. Dirty, rust-stained patches of ice were all that was left behind.

Katu lifted up his cloak to check on the king underneath.

'He's still alive,' he said, replacing the cloak. 'But we need to get him back to the palace quickly. Our only hope is that the *Nightjar* will reach us in time. We need to find the others before they—'

A sudden rustle from the next mountainside, somewhere just below the harpoon guns, made them duck.

'Quickly,' Katu whispered. 'Get behind the cage.'

They all crouched low and ducked behind, their bodies hidden by the great bulk of the king. Katu peered above. There was the sound of footsteps running, loose rocks clattering. Whoever it was was very close. Jackson watched Katu's eyes narrow and then grow wide. He stood up, grabbing on to the cage to support his injured leg. 'It's OK, look!'

Jackson came out from behind the cage, grinning when he saw Sparks and Lotti running down the valley. He gave Sparks a hug and then looked over her shoulder, sure he would see Zeina just behind them.

'Where's Zeina?' he asked Sparks.

She shook her head, tears pooling in her eyes.

'She never came back,' she whispered.

'What do you mean, Sparks?' Jackson asked a little louder than he meant to. Lotti came forward, placing a paw on Jackson's arm.

'The lawkeepers panicked when the power went out. I was worried they might use the harpoons against the whales but they were far more concerned about saving their own skins. I left Sparks and Zeina to fix the solar tech to the echophone machine and they did a wonderful job.' She smiled reassuringly at Sparks. 'But Zeina heard pistol fire and went to investigate – Sparks waited and waited, but Zeina never returned.'

'I'm sorry,' Sparks whispered close to Jackson's ear. 'I should have stopped her.'

'It's not your fault, Sparks,' Jackson said, ashamed that he had been so brisk. He knew only too well that trying to stop Zeina from doing anything was a lost cause.

'Wait, is that an ice raven?' Shrapnel called, taking off Hamilton's ridiculous top hat to better see. He pointed towards a flash of icy light that paused in mid-air just above them, materialising into a beautiful white bird. It swooped down to rest on Katu's shoulder. Albi croaked urgently and then took off again, flying towards the mountain that Sparks and Lotti had just descended from. He hovered, circling and cawing impatiently. Katu and Lotti exchanged worried looks.

'What is it?' Jackson demanded. 'Does he know where Zeina is?'

'He's warning us she's in danger,' Katu said quietly, watching the skies with narrowed eyes.

'What kind of danger?' Shrapnel urged. 'Where is she? Ask him!'

'It's not quite as simple as that,' Lotti replied. 'We don't communicate with him in sentences. It's more like a sense or a feeling. Katu knows him better; just give him a second.'

261

Katu was frowning, watching and listening to Albi as he darted and circled.

'It's Steele,' he growled. 'Steele has her.'

'Where?' Shrapnel and Jackson demanded in unison.

'Somewhere in the sky,' Katu snarled, his eyes scouring the great blue expanse behind Albi. 'An airship.'

And then Jackson spotted it. A stream of smoke just above the mountaintop. It rose – funnels, pistons, a shining glass cockpit and then the black-and-silver-striped hull of an airship. He reeled – it was the *Raven*! Or at least a smaller version of the *Raven*. It was turning, heading north and away from them.

Jackson wasted no time. Glancing back at the grey smoke from the mine, he retrieved his aerocycle from his backpack.

'Jackson,' Katu called, limping over to try and stop him. 'It's too dangerous. We should wait; the *Nightjar* will be here soon. She won't get away, I promise.'

Jackson shrugged him off – he didn't have a plan exactly but he knew he had to get to that airship. He had left Hamilton. He would not let Steele take Zeina. Zeina would do exactly the same for him. She *had* done exactly the same for him.

He started to run, Shrapnel following behind.

'Wait, Jackson, I'm coming too!'

Jackson stopped, unfolded his aerocycle and hopped on. In a matter of seconds he was joined by Shrapnel, who jumped on the back.

'Is this thing even going to fly?' he asked, wrapping his arms round Jackson's waist.

'I'm not sure. This one still has its smog chamber attached. Hopefully the smog in the atmosphere from that mine will be enough.'

Together, they jumped, Jackson pedalling as hard as he could, and just as Lotti and Katu reached them, WHOOSH! up they sailed into the air.

Jackson looked down, but only for a second. Lotti waved frantically. Katu was shouting something after him – something he couldn't hear. He turned and concentrated instead on the *Raven II*, pedalling as fast as he could. Every few seconds the smog chamber would stutter and they would drop suddenly, before it kicked back in. Jackson just hoped there was enough smog to keep them in the air long enough to reach the airship.

'She's getting away!' Shrapnel called over the wind.

'I'm going as fast as I can,' Jackson grunted, his legs burning.

Shrapnel was right – the stripes of the rounded hull were getting smaller rather than larger as the airship rose and accelerated.

Then, without warning, the *Raven II* swerved, turning back towards the mountain, back towards Jackson and Shrapnel.

As the starboard side came into view, Jackson noticed something hanging from the decking – a person, legs writhing, desperately hanging on to the railings. The legs were far too long to belong to Zeina and yet it definitely wasn't Steele either.

'It's Nedra!' Shrapnel cried in horror. 'Come on, Jackson, she's going to fall—She's going to—'

He yelled as Nedra's body fell from the airship to the mountain below. There was nothing they could do to catch her. They were still too far away. Jackson watched as Nedra slumped down the mountainside. A figure stood up and walked away from the railings – someone tall with long auburn hair that blew in the wind. Steele.

The *Raven II* lurched again, turning back in a circle away from them. The unmistakeable figure of Zeina came into view, her black curls swept against her face, as she leaned over the railings to see where Nedra had fallen.

'We can do it, Shrapnel,' Jackson yelled, his voice cracking. 'We can get to her in time.'

The changes of direction had slowed the *Raven II* enough so that now they were gaining on it – but Jackson knew that it would only be a minute or two before the airship reached full speed again. Jackson pedalled with all the energy he had left, every muscle working at full capacity. The deck of the airship drifted closer and closer. He watched Zeina spot them. She looked oddly serene as she climbed over the railings.

'Hold on,' Jackson yelled. 'Hold on!'

He watched in horror as she let go with one arm, her hand dancing in the icy breeze.

'She's going to jump!' Shrapnel called.

Panic shot through Jackson's heart – what if they couldn't catch her? What if she dropped to the mountaintop, like Nedra?

They were metres away – no, more.

'Get ready, Shrapnel. You'll have to catch her!'

Jackson swooped up and turned so that Shrapnel would be parallel with Zeina.

'What? No, I can't!' Shrapnel cried.

'We don't have a choice, Shrapnel! She's going to jump anyway!'

They were so close now that he could hear Zeina counting. ONE. TWO. THREE.

And she jumped.

Jackson pedalled, turning sharply so that the back of the aerocycle would be as close as possible. He felt Shrapnel lean away from him, grabbing out to reach Zeina as she fell through the air.

For one horrible second he thought that they'd missed—but then the aerocycle lurched downwards.

Jackson risked a glance, spotting Zeina half on, half off, her arms around Shrapnel's waist. His arms gripped under hers, holding her up, but her legs were dangling in the air. The extra weight had pushed the aerocycle off balance and there was nothing Jackson could do now but try to slow the fall.

He turned the handlebars out of the tailspin, desperately trying to pedal upwards against the gravity that was pulling them at great speed to the mountaintop.

CHAPTER 29

'Urgh.' Zeina sat up, rubbing her throbbing head with aching arms. Her hair was a twisted mess of twigs and debris. Dazed, it took her a second to remember where she was.

Jackson had managed to pull the aerocycle up enough so that they had landed with a skid rather than a crash, but Zeina still had rips in her overalls and deep grazes to her shins where her bottom half had scraped along the rocks. Her feet had been saved by her thick winter boots.

Shrapnel and Jackson were beginning to stir around her, groaning and stretching their limbs cautiously. Other than a few more cuts and bruises to add to their collections, thankfully both seemed to have escaped their crash-landing relatively unscathed.

'What in heavens, Zee!' Shrapnel groaned. 'You can't just jump off a moving airship and expect us to catch you.'

'I didn't have a choice!' Zeina replied, brushing a mixture of mud and snow from her hair and coat. 'I wasn't going to be taken as a hostage.'

'It was stupid and reckless, Zeina,' Jackson grumbled as she helped him to his feet. 'You could have died.'

'But I knew you would make it,' she replied, squeezing Jackson tightly. 'And I knew *you* would catch me,' she added, hugging Shrapnel too.

'Now, we need to get to Ned,' Shrapnel said, his eyes darting across the mountaintop. 'She could be—Let's just find her, quickly. It'll be down this way somewhere.'

Shrapnel took off down the mountainside before Zeina could explain.

'Wait, Shrapnel, there's something you need to know—'

Zeina and Jackson followed Shrapnel as he raced down the narrow track, weaving in and out of jagged rocks, jumping over the roots of trees. It took them only a few minutes to find her, right on the very edge of an exposed outcrop. The outcrop was held together by the roots of a tree that gripped on to the mountain desperately. With the force of Nedra's fall, some of the ground beneath her had already begun to landslide down the mountain – Zeina could see loose earth, black against the snow. Some of the tree roots Nedra was balanced on now twisted into nothing.

Shrapnel wasted no time in jumping down on to the outcrop and edging over to where Nedra lay unconscious.

'Shrapnel!' Zeina called.

The earth under Nedra's body shuddered. More rocks began to break away from the tree roots and tumbled down the mountainside. Shrapnel retreated, not wanting to cause the whole outcrop to give way entirely.

But the movement beneath her had drawn Nedra back to consciousness. Her eyes opened wide, taking in Zeina, Jackson, Shrapnel, the unstable outcrop and the tree that cradled her body. She panicked, flipping over on to her front and desperately trying to get up on to all fours.

The tree trunk began to tip away from the mountain, taking its roots, the earth and Nedra with it.

'Ah!' Nedra screamed.

They all leapt forward, teetering on the last stable part of the outcrop, while the tree toppled forward and tumbled down the mountain.

Zeina felt a hand grip her elbow desperately and she grabbed on to Nedra's elbow in turn. Nedra's other hand had found Shrapnel's, and now that the outcrop had gone completely, Zeina and Shrapnel's grip was the only thing preventing Nedra from crashing down the mountainside. For the second time Zeina watched Nedra's legs swing, desperately trying to find some foothold so that she could scramble up.

'Don't let go!' she pleaded. 'Please don't let go!' Her tears flowed, making clear trails down her dirt-scraped cheeks.

Zeina shook her head. 'We won't, I promise.'

Jackson leaned forward as far as he could, trying to catch at her clothes, find anything that he could grab to help Nedra haul herself to safety. Her legs scrambled desperately.

'I'm sorry,' Ned cried. 'I was wrong about her, Zeina. I'm so sorry.'

Shrapnel frowned. Jackson looked at Zeina, perplexed. But Zeina shook her head at them – there would be time for explanations later.

'Jackson, go and get the aerocycle. You'll have to fly down and help push her up from below. Quickly!' Zeina groaned. She now had hold of Nedra's arm with both of hers. A gnawing pain was creeping up into her neck and shoulders; she wasn't sure how much longer she could hold on. She heard Jackson's feet thundering back up the mountain pass – she hoped that the aerocycle would fly. She leaned back, putting all her weight into holding Nedra up.

'It was me, Zeina,' Nedra cried. 'I'm sorry. She had me in some kind of frenzy. I was so angry.'

'It doesn't matter, Nedra, not now,' Zeina said firmly. She knew what it was like to be under Steele's spell, to have such faith in her that it blinded you.

'But you don't understand,' Nedra sobbed. 'It was me. I damaged that chandelier . . . I wanted it to fall on you – to hurt you. And then it hurt Shrapnel and Katu instead. And . . . I was so angry with you.'

Shrapnel recoiled in horror, his hand slipping slightly. Nedra screamed and he caught her again.

'Please don't let go. I'm sorry – I'm so, so sorry.'

'None of that matters right now, Nedra,' Zeina said, her voice shaking. 'Just hold on. Jackson will be here soon.'

Zeina looked away. At that moment she couldn't process what Nedra had just admitted to them – she had to focus on just holding on. The sun was full in the sky; the *Nightjar* had to be here soon.

But, casting her eyes skywards, her heart sank. She saw the black and silver stripes coming back towards them.

'It's Steele,' Zeina cried. 'She's coming back!'

Nedra cried desperately. Her body went limp, like she was giving up. Her hand loosened on Zeina's elbow. 'Leave me! You have to let go. You have to run!'

'We aren't letting go, Ned,' Shrapnel said gruffly. He was crying too. Zeina couldn't remember the last time she had seen him cry.

The hull of the *Raven II* grew larger and larger, casting a dark shadow across the sun. It was heading straight for them. Was Steele angry enough to fire those harpoons at them,

271

Zeina wondered? Or would she finish Nedra off and then take them all as hostages? Instead of saving herself by jumping from that airship, maybe Zeina had just endangered her friends.

The whirr of a smaller propeller signalled that, at last, Jackson had arrived. The aerocycle lurched and weaved. It was in desperate need of repairs, Zeina thought, but for now it just needed to fly a few moments longer.

Jackson groaned, wrestling with the handlebars until it flew in the direction he wanted. Zeina watched his mouth open wide with panic as he saw the *Raven II*, now no more than thirty metres from them. Jackson swooped up from under Nedra's feet. Zeina looked down, watching him pedal frantically while pushing up her legs with his shoulder, giving Nedra just enough strength to find a foothold at last. Zeina and Shrapnel pulled backwards with all their might and Nedra managed to push herself up so that her chest now rested on the outcrop edge.

'One more, Ned,' Shrapnel shouted.

Zeina and Shrapnel hooked their arms round her torso, pulling as Jackson pushed up. Nedra roared as she hauled herself to safety, with Jackson following closely behind.

WHOOSH.

The sound of a harpoon sliced through the air. It struck the rocks where, only seconds before, Nedra's feet had swung.

What was left of the outcrop rumbled and the four of them huddled together, as close to the mountainside as they could. The path had collapsed – there was nowhere left to run.

Zeina felt Nedra's wet cheeks pressing into neck, Jackson's hand tight in hers, Shrapnel's arms wrapped around them all as if he could protect them from the strike that was about to come.

WHOOSH.

Zeina's eyes screwed shut – ready for the sound of metal on rock, ready for the earth to crumble beneath her, ready for the fall.

But it didn't come.

'It's Parr!' Jackson cried, releasing Zeina's hand to point into the sky. 'The *Nightjar*! Look!'

The *Nightjar* sailed towards them like a beautiful bird. Steele's harpoon had missed its target and clattered into the valley below, and as the *Nightjar* advanced, the *Raven II* began to turn.

'Why is she retreating?' Zeina asked.

'She hasn't got a crew,' Nedra said quietly. 'She can't fly and reload the harpoons all by herself. She has nobody now.'

They watched as the *Nightjar* gave chase, its wings soaring across the blue sky. Underneath, every single one of the cycles was in use. Puffing and panting, Beard's red face smiled down at them.

'Any news on that solar tech, Zeina?' he called down, laughing. Zeina waved back.

Behind the *Nightjar*, just below its tail-shaped rudder, buzzed the four short-range airships. The *Pine Hawk* swooped down with her dad at the helm. His eyes were full of tears as he helped each of them in turn from the rocks to the safety of the ship.

'Oh, Zeina,' he cried. 'I've been so worried.'

STEELE SENTENCED

In an amazing turn of events, infamous explorer Vivianne Steele, who was presumed dead, has been sentenced by the Court of the Emerald King to life imprisonment in Palik's high-security prison, Geldina Dungeon. The facility, located inside the heart of a frozen mountain, is reserved for the most dangerous criminals of the Northern Continent, many of whom will never see the outside world again.

On the day of the spring Equinox, Steele was captured by the Smog Rats and later arrested by the Emerald King's National Guard. Last week, the court of the Feln King found Steele guilty of numerous crimes including: attempted murder, kidnapping, embezzlement, animal cruelty and espionage. Steele's life sentence is without parole.

The true nature of her company, Osiris, has shocked Belows and Aboves alike. Many Aboves who

275

invested in the technology have found themselves losing millions on the stock market. Indeed, this week has seen a fresh spate of bankruptcy announcements. Along with the rising cost of ore, there is now also a shortage of STANS technology, following the complete destruction of the illegal northern facility and the death of their head scientist, Dr Giles Mortwell.

It might have been a very different story were it not for the brave actions of a small group of Smog Rats. The incident has solidified efforts across the continents to combat the evil STANS technology. A new alliance had been drafted between the Smog Rats, the Kotarth and the Feln, which prohibits the use of such technology and any ore-powered airships across the Western and Northern Continents.

Of course, lawmakers and lawkeepers will continue to do everything they can to fight back. Life for Belows in cities on the Eastern Continent is becoming harder by the day. Efforts must now be focused on rescuing the sky whales that remain slaves to their STAN systems, as well as uniting to rescue the Belows still imprisoned in the mines that remain under Above control. As always, this

publication's message to you is to STAY STRONG.
The change is coming. May we all have the courage
to do what we know is right.

Pseudonym

===

CHAPTER 30

'You're sure you want to see her?' Jackson asked, watching his friend tremble slightly as they approached the notorious Geldina Dungeon.

'I'm sure,' Zeina nodded, chin raised, eyes taking in the enormity of the iron doors set into the frozen mountain.

She stepped forward and pulled the bell. A tiny hatch slid open and a pair of fierce eyes blinked back at them.

'Yes?' an irritable voice growled.

'Zeina Starborn and Jackson Willoughby,' Zeina said. 'The king has given us his permission to visit.'

The eyes disappeared, the hatch slammed shut and then the doors creaked open.

Inside, the dungeon was lit only by lamps that smoked with the stench of burning blubber. It felt so strange to Jackson to be surrounded by darkness again. During the two weeks they had spent recovering in the Glacial Palace, the days of Valco Sol had grown longer and longer and for the last few nights the sun hadn't set at all. They were moved from the Glacial Palace, as it soon would begin to melt, and had a few days in Palik City while the last preparations were made to both the *Nightjar* and the *Osprey*. Last week Zeina's dad had flown over to bring the new ship north. After tomorrow's ceremony the two airships would be ready to leave. One heading south and the other going east. Jackson still didn't know which he would be on.

The dungeon guard gestured down a dingy corridor. 'She's down that way,' he snarled. 'Last cell on the left. You've got two minutes, no more.'

'Are you sure you want to do this, Zeina?' Jackson asked again. 'She did . . . you know . . . try to kill you . . .'

'I'm sure,' his brave friend replied.

They passed cell after cell, each one dank, gloomy and secured by thick iron bars. Many were unoccupied, or at least appeared so. But every so often a pair of eyes would glare dangerously at them from the dark.

The last cell on the left also appeared empty at first.

Zeina approached the bars. 'Hello?' she whispered.

'Zeina, Jackson,' a voice replied. 'I didn't think you'd come.'

Stepping into the glow from the lamp-lit corridor, a face appeared at the bars. Her grey eyes blinked at them both. Her short, fuzzy hair had grown longer and shaggy in places. She smiled, and Jackson was glad she seemed to have shed the haunted look she had when he'd seen the Feln guards take her away.

'Nedra,' Zeina smiled, holding her hand out through the bars for Nedra to take.

This worried Jackson – just a few weeks ago, Nedra had tried to kill Zeina. But as the two girls held hands, he saw nothing but warmth between them.

'Shrapnel?' Nedra asked hopefully.

'He . . . couldn't come . . .' Zeina replied.

Nedra sighed. 'I deceived him worst of all, I suppose. I used him to get close to you. And he was so kind and welcoming.'

'You were upset when the chandelier injured him,' Zeina said gently.

'I was,' Nedra replied. 'That was genuine. At the time, I didn't care that I had hurt Katu – Steele had poisoned me with awful things about him. But I genuinely cared for Shrapnel. I still do,' she smiled sadly. 'And I was so angry with you, Zeina. It was my attempt to hurt you that had hurt him.' She shook her head. 'It all seems so strange now that I've had time to think. I was full of rage. Steele was the one who had rescued me from the mining grounds when I thought there was nobody left to come. She had said such terrible things about you and I believed them all.' Nedra sniffed. 'She said I was special to her and that we would go on great adventures together. And I had been so lonely for such a long time. Then when I heard her spewing the same lies to you on that airship, it all became clear to me. She doesn't care about anyone but herself.'

'She used you. It's what she does. She took advantage of you when you were at your most vulnerable and turned you against everyone else.'

Nedra nodded, wiping her tears away angrily, her eyes glinting. 'Are you going to visit *her* too?'

'We can't, even if we wanted to,' said Zeina. 'She's in the highest-security part of the dungeon – right in the centre of the mountain. No one goes in or out. And she'll be there until . . . for ever.'

'It's still too good for her,' Nedra spat. 'What about Sparks, didn't she want to see me either?'

'She did,' Jackson said. 'But she was, err, needed . . .' He trailed off uselessly.

Parr had warned them not to say a thing to Nedra about the airships, or the solar tech, or about any of the Smog Rats' plans for the future. Sparks was busy with Lotti, finishing off the wiring for the solar tech on the *Osprey*.

Nedra's eyes sparkled. 'Fitting that amazing new technology of Zeina's to all the Smog Rats' airships, I heard? And you're both to receive medals from the king at tomorrow's celebration?'

Zeina and Jackson turned to each other, incredulous.

Nedra laughed. 'Once a spy, always a spy.' She shrugged. 'There's whispers all down the corridor about it. Congratulations. You both deserve it entirely. And I,' she sighed, casting her eyes towards the dank ceiling of her cell, 'I deserve *this* entirely.'

Zeina frowned. 'How long did you get?' she asked.

'A year in here.' Nedra looked around glumly. 'But I could get out sooner if I behave myself. Parr managed to get some of the charges dropped and so it was just theft and espionage in the end.'

Jackson nodded. It was in fact Zeina who had insisted the more serious charge of attempted murder be dropped. Parr had simply gone along with it.

'It could be worse – this place is almost luxurious after the mining grounds!' she smiled weakly. 'After here, I have to serve five years working for the Emerald King himself, paying back my debt to society, and then I'm free. Once I'm released, I'd like more than anything to come back to the Smog Rats. After the spell Steele had me under was broken, I realised that I had everything that I was looking for already. I had found my family. Put in a good word for me with Parr, won't you?'

As her tears fell, Jackson's heart began to ache, for he knew what it was like to find family with the Smog Rats after feeling so lonely for so long. Speaking of Parr, he thought it very unlikely that she would ever trust Nedra to come back to them.

'You're not Pseudonym then?' Jackson sighed.

It had the desired effect; Nedra began to cackle.

'No, I'm not Pseudonym.' She smiled, wiping her tears away. 'I suspected that you two believed I was, and I let you. It provided me with the cover I needed to send messages to Steele.'

'You don't know who is, do you?' Zeina asked tentatively.

'You still don't know?!' Nedra exclaimed.

Both Jackson and Zeina shook their heads.

'Well then, it isn't for me to give them away but, *yes*, I have my suspicions.' Her eyes sparkled mischievously.

'Two minutes are up!' the guard huffed, lumbering down the corridor, spear in paw. 'Hey!' He clunked the spear across the bars, making Zeina and Nedra spring apart. 'Away from the bars,' he roared at Nedra. 'Time's up! You two, out!'

Before they were ushered out, Zeina ran up to the bars once more and grabbed Nedra's hand. She whispered something and Jackson was sure he saw a small shining object of some kind pass between them.

'HEY,' roared the guard. 'I SAID OUT. NOW!'

'What did you give her?' Jackson whispered as they were

shoved unceremoniously out of the iron doors, blinking in the sunlight reflecting brightly off the white snow.

'After Nedra was arrested, I found both the whale brooches in my coat pocket,' Zeina smiled. 'Nedra must have slipped them in there, just before she was seized by the king's guards.'

'You gave her back her tracking device!' Jackson exclaimed, imagining the trouble they would both be in if Parr ever found out.

'No,' Zeina smiled again, 'I gave her my purple brooch and I've kept Nedra's red one. I told her that once she was free, I would come and find her.'

CHAPTER 31

The streets of Palik hummed. Feln, young and old alike, filled the terraces, balconies, windows and doorways – anywhere they could get a good view of the parade that weaved through the streets to the city square. Flags of emerald fluttered in the gentle breeze and golden decorations of the sun and moon glinted in the sunlight. After their spring Equinox celebrations had been cancelled, everyone was determined to enjoy this day.

Zeina smiled and waved. Ahead of her marched Commander Hugrak, Katu and Captain Parr, holding their flagpoles high. On each flag was the new symbol of the alliance – a blue sky whale and a white one with horns, circling each other within an emerald sun. Jackson was shaking slightly as he marched next to her.

'You'll be OK!' Zeina whispered.

'The crowd is enormous,' Jackson said through gritted teeth. 'What if I go red and freeze up?'

'You won't!' she replied. 'We'll all be up there with you.'

She watched Shrapnel, just a little behind, smiling and waving at the crowd in his new uniform. He had spent another week in the infirmary after they were rescued but now his cheek had healed, leaving just the shadow of a scar. Sparks trotted next to him, the same emblem of the whales and sun proudly displayed on her puffed-out chest.

The city square was a large platform cut into the black mountainside. On three sides were windows and balconies, all richly decorated and teeming with faces. At the centre was a large stage with a black throne. The king was helped to his feet as the parade arrived to fill the square. He wore a new cloak with the symbol of the alliance embroidered on to it. The magnificent Emerald Crown shone on his head, and yet he seemed smaller and humble. His black eyes welcomed them with nothing but kindness. After they had got him back to the Glacial Palace, he had been rushed to the hospital wing and for the first few days nobody knew whether he would make it at all.

'My fellow Feln and our new friends, I welcome you all to this momentous occasion!' he bellowed.

A cheer rang around the square.

'After the spring Equinox celebrations were so *rudely* interrupted, it is amazing that now we can celebrate two occasions at once. As well as greeting the return of the sun, today we can welcome in a new beginning for the Feln,

Kotarth and Smog Rats. A time where we will work together in trust and friendship, sharing information, resources and technology. Our objective is clear – to rid our world of the STAN system and the power Above families hold over us. No more will we stand apart, watching them pollute and destroy our world. United we can beat them and build a new world with a bright future!'

Another cheer erupted from the crowds as the Emerald King was joined by Katu and Captain Parr. They held hands and paws, holding them up in the air, victorious in the roar of applause.

'Today I can announce four joint initiatives that will begin straight away. The first is the Alliance Force, a defence force made up of humans, Feln and Kotarth, united in their aims to liberate the last of the mining grounds and protect us all from Above lawkeepers.'

He paused a moment, while the crowds cheered.

'The second is the Alliance Safe Zone, an area of land spanning from here in Palik, west over the mountains and liberated mining grounds, and south-west to the Kotarth Forest. This zone will be secured by our forces, both over land and in the air. A route to share resources and workforce. An area where ore-powered airships and technology are banned. The third is a new airship factory, built here in Palik on the site we reclaimed from Steele. Our airships will be made only from scrap metal and powered only by renewable technology. The best innovators from across our lands will come together here to develop and invent new forms of power.'

Zeina's stomach fluttered – she was certain her dad would be asked to stay behind and help Lotti set up the airship factory.

'The fourth is our Alliance Outreach, captained by our friend Penelope Parr. She will lead the way with her two solar-powered airships the *Nightjar* and the *Osprey*, continuing their work to free the last of the sky whale hotels across the Eastern and Southern Continents and attempting to make contact with the last of our lost cousins, the Zugmi.'

Zeina watched Jackson as he cheered for Parr. She didn't know where Jackson, Sparks and Shrapnel would end up but she was certain it wouldn't be here at the airship factory. Could she leave her dad and go with them? Would she even be given that chance? She pushed the thoughts to the back of her head. First they had to get through the medal ceremony.

'For too long we have hidden; now is the time to fight!' the king continued to the biggest roar from the crowd yet. 'And now there are a few thanks I must give. May I please have Lotti, Shrapnel, Jackson, Zeina and Sparks to the stage.'

Jackson flushed instantly.

'Come on,' Zeina said, grabbing his clammy hand in hers. They positioned themselves in a line across the stage, Katu stepping forward to join them.

'These beings thought nothing of risking their lives to save others. They showed courage,' the king bent down to pin a gold medal with emerald ribbon tails to Shrapnel's chest, 'empathy,' he continued, smiling down at Jackson, 'ingenuity,' Lotti winked at him as he pinned her medal, 'strength,' Sparks beamed, 'resilience,' Katu gave the king a little bow, 'and sacrifice.' Zeina felt the cool weight of the medal as it was pinned to her uniform. She moved it in the sunlight, watching the engraved alliance emblem shimmer.

'It is to them that we owe our security and I owe my life,' the king continued, tears gathering at the corners of his black eyes. 'And now, without further ado, let the celebrations begin!'

Another cheer erupted and a band of Feln started up their instruments with a merry tune. Large tables were laid out in the square, laden with a mouth-watering feast of all the foods that had become Zeina's favourites in the weeks they had spent on the Northern Continent. She watched as the king poured lilaberry wine into a tankard for Captain Parr, Shrapnel reached across the table for one of Sparks's favourite pastries, and Katu and Lotti smiled and laughed together. She should feel happy, but instead, now the excitement of the medal ceremony was over, she felt a little empty.

'What is it, Zeina?' her father asked, putting an arm around her shoulder.

'It's just . . . what happens now?' she asked. 'They'll want innovators to stay here and help with the new airship factory, I suppose?'

'It's likely.'

'But Parr will want Sparks and Jackson to stay with her? And I suppose Shrapnel will want to join the Alliance Force? And Katu – he's been away from his home for such a long time.'

Her father nodded again. Zeina's heart sank. 'Does that mean . . . we'll all be split up?'

'Come on,' he said. 'It's time we told you all, I think.'

He signalled to Parr, who whispered to Katu, and together they rounded up Shrapnel, Sparks and Jackson. Captain Parr ushered them all together and bustled them down an alley away from the hubbub. It led through the mountain and then round to the platform where the *Nightjar* was moored. The sight of the *Nightjar*'s wings filled Zeina with the same amazement that they had that first time, when it rescued her from Steele's ship. To her, this airship would always be a symbol of hope and family. It didn't matter how many other airships she was asked to build in Palik – the *Nightjar* would always be her home.

'It's time I shared our plans with you.' Parr sighed heavily. Zeina's stomach dropped as she looked at her friends' anxious faces – she couldn't bear it. She looked down instead at the frozen ground.

'I know you have been wondering where you are all going next. I apologise that I had to hold you in suspense but certain things had to be finalised. As you know, the two airships will tackle the Eastern and Southern Continents separately. The *Osprey* will now go east and I will captain the *Nightjar*, which will go south.'

Jackson's eyebrows raised, he turned to Zeina who tried her best to smile – Jackson would get to go south, just like he had wanted. Part of Zeina wanted to run back to the party. She wasn't sure she could hear Parr say that she and her dad would have to stay behind. It made her feel sick thinking about being away from her friends, having that worry gnaw away at her.

Parr fixed her steadily with her eye. It was clear that their captain was certain in her decision. Zeina reminded herself that Captain Parr always made decisions with their best interests in mind. This alliance was what Parr had been trying to achieve all along and she had been right – it had made them all safer. The captain had never given Zeina a reason to doubt her decisions. It was thanks to her that she and Jackson had been rescued from Steele in the first place, and that her dad and Shrapnel had been saved from the Western Mountains. Parr had given them all a home and a family and a cause to fight for.

Right then, Zeina decided that whatever Parr said, she could take it. Whatever she needed her to do, she would do it.

'There have been developments that mean I will need a few more crew members to come south with us than I had originally planned,' Parr said slowly, holding up a document that Zeina could not read, for the paper was so old and the handwriting so faded and loopy.

'These are the deeds for some land that the Kotarth have gifted to the Smog Rats. It forms part of the alliance – because at the moment, you see, we have no land of our own. It was land given to the Kotarth by the Zugmi a hundred generations ago. A little pocket where the Southern Continent meets the west. As you know, the Southern Continent was made uninhabitable by human pollution many years ago. It's burning and barren. All contact has been lost with the Zugmi, if there are even any left to be found.'

'Come on, Parr!' called Shrapnel impatiently. 'Enough of the history lesson, just tell us what we're doing!' Sparks began to giggle. Parr rolled her eye and smiled.

'We are going to build on this land, Shrapnel. A secret solar city. Somewhere we can experiment with how to make the land habitable again. Somewhere we can use as a base to tackle the sky whale hotels on the southern tourist route.'

'Won't it be dangerous?' Jackson asked. 'There's lawkeepers on the Southern Continent.'

'It's as dangerous as anything else we've done,' Parr shrugged, her eye sparkling. 'But if we succeed, it will be somewhere to build from. I'll be taking a large team, which can include all of you – Shrapnel as our link to the spy network; Katu to lead the outreach mission to find the Zugmi; Asher and Zeina to build the city, inventing new ways to make energy and pump water.' Parr turned to Jackson, beaming with pride. 'Jackson – Jamie was so impressed by how you removed the STAN system from that whale, he's insisting on training you up to be his deputy.'

Jackson flushed but looked pleased.

'Is that right, Dad?' Zeina turned to him. 'We can *both* go? You're not needed here at the airship factory?'

'Lotti is going to be in charge here,' he smiled. 'So yes, we can both go – that's if it's what you want?'

Zeina nodded vigorously, hugging her friends.

'Hey, what about Sparks?' she asked, noticing her standing a little away from them, her hands fiddling nervously.

'Ah, yes, Sparks! Sparks is going to be in charge of our radio communications and . . . news.'

'News?' queried Jackson.

'Yes, news,' Parr repeated, frowning slightly. She gave Sparks a curt nod.

Sparks stepped forward, staring down at the ground. She took a deep breath – Zeina wasn't sure she had seen her speak out loud in front of this many people before.

'I'm . . . Pseudonym,' she said.

'WHAT?' Jackson and Zeina exclaimed, their mouths falling open.

Sparks wouldn't look them in the eye. They turned to Parr, who somehow seemed both disapproving and proud at the same time.

'Aren't you angry?' Zeina asked.

'I was,' Parr grunted. 'But Sparks and I have talked it through. I can see why she did what she did.'

'It started as a way to share my ideas,' Sparks piped up. 'The ones I couldn't say out loud.'

'You lied to us?' Zeina said before she could stop herself. Jackson elbowed her in the ribs.

'I never lied.' Sparks stared back, unflinching. 'I just didn't say.'

'How did you do it, Sparks?' Jackson asked. 'Finding out all the information and then getting it printed and delivered across the continents?'

'I had a little help . . .' She smiled shyly at Shrapnel, who gave her a little salute in return.

'YOU?' Zeina cried, turning to stare at Shrapnel, an irritating smugness playing about his lips.

'Yes, me. No need to be so surprised, Zee,' he chuckled. 'I'm a boy of many talents. You are looking at the one and only secret reporter.'

Parr cleared her throat pointedly and Shrapnel shrank a little.

'What about the king?' Jackson asked Parr tentatively. 'Won't he want to see Sparks arrested when he finds out? Doesn't it put the alliance in danger?'

'The king knows,' Parr replied. 'And after a long discussion and an apology from Sparks, he agrees with me. Both of us can see now that we have to spread our message across the four continents every chance we get. The *Smog Scoop* has proved *very* successful and the alliance will need a newspaper to distribute across the Safe Zone and to Belows trapped in eastern cities. Sparks can write it from the south, but now she will have a network of reporters from all over the alliance.'

Zeina turned to Sparks. The initial anger at being kept in the dark had disappeared and what was left was nothing but pride for her clever friend. Sparks held out her hands – one to Jackson and the other to Zeina. They hugged her and Shrapnel came and wrapped his arms around them too. From inside their huddle Sparks's voice rang out, loud and clear.

'We won't stay silent in the smog any more.'

ACKNOWLEDGEMENTS

It has been a joy to write this second instalment of Zeina and Jackson's story and I must thank an extensive cast of incredibly supportive characters, without which *Zeina Starborn and the Emerald King* would not have been possible.

First and foremost I must thank my brilliant agent, Chloe Seager. I am forever grateful for your expertise, honesty and kindness. Thank you also to Maddy Belton and to everyone at the Madeleine Milburn Literary Agency, who have been so supportive throughout my journey into the world of publishing.

Zeina Starborn and the Emerald King would certainly not be the book it is today without the incredible editorial powers of Nazima Abdillahi. Thank you Nazima – I felt so privileged to have you as my editor, for this, our second, adventure together into the world of Zeina Starborn! Thank you to all the wonderful people at Hachette Children's Group who have been so supportive at each stage of the publication process, including (but certainly not limited to) Ruth Girmatsion, Hazel Cotton, Sarah Farmer, Katie Maxwell, Dominic Kingston and Tig Wallace.

Thank you so much to the very talented Michelle Brackenborough for the cover design and to George Ermos for his beautiful cover illustration. I receive so many compliments about the extraordinary covers of both *Zeina Starborn* books and I feel very lucky to have the world I created represented in such a way.

Winning the Northern Writers' Awards by New Writing North is what started this journey and I am supremely thankful for their continued support. Thank you for promoting writers in the North of England and for introducing me to my Northern Writers' family – James Harris, Andy Ruffell and Karon Alderman.

In the last two years, I have been fortunate to meet many booksellers, book reviewers, bloggers and fellow authors, both online and in person, who have been so generous and welcoming. Thank you to all who have championed *Zeina Starborn* – you are an amazing group of people, without which none of this would be possible.

Following the publication of *Zeina Starborn and the Sky Whale,* I was blown away by the support of my friends, family and colleagues. I feel fortunate to have a support network that have been there for me through the highs and lows of life and I feel blessed to be able to celebrate this achievement with them. Thank you to my husband, Kieron, for your constant faith in me, my children, for being my inspiration and my parents and in-laws, for your constant support. A special shout-out must go to Michael Durkan, who is always the first person I send any writing to – thank you for your kind honesty (and extensive feedback notes!). Thank you also to all the staff and pupils at Valley View Community Primary School, who have been so supportive and excited about the publication of this book.

Finally and most importantly, I must thank YOU, the person reading this book. Thank you for choosing to go on another adventure with Zeina and Jackson. I hope their story inspires you to explore your world, trust your instincts and fight for the causes (and people) that you hold dear.